Cryptoanomaly

Written by David A. Lyons

Book Two in the Synced Series

Written by: David A. Lyons

ISBN: 979-8-9927564-4-9

This is not a story. It is a correction.

Published by Vehemently Inked LLC

Preface
7

Introduction
9

Prologue
11

Chapter 1 - The Night the City Was
13

Chapter 2 - The Algorithm of the Inevitable
31

Chapter 3 - Beneath the Architect's Design
51

Chapter 4 - Marked for Later
77

Chapter 5 - The Ethics of Correction
95

Chapter 6 - The Echo Within the Absence
115

Chapter 7 - The Hand That Shapes
125

Chapter 8 - The Moment It Recognized You
141

Chapter 9 - Point of No Return
161

Chapter 10 – Residual Code
177

Chapter 11 - The Protocol Beneath Memory
189

Chapter 12 - Threats That Rewrite Themselves
201

Chapter 13 - Redemption Is a Loop
207

Chapter 14 - Whispers in the System
213

Chapter 15 - Eclipsing the Clockwork Mind
217

Chapter 16 - Where the Rewrite Begins
221

Chapter 17: The Flow Beyond Recognition
233

Preface

Cryptoanomoly began as a spark in a world increasingly tethered to technology's promises and perils. This story is not a prediction but a mirror, reflecting questions we face today: What does it mean to be human when our minds can be edited like code? How do we hold onto truth in a reality that shifts beneath us? The tale of New Haven, it's people, and the shadow of Chronosync is fiction, yet it draws from the tensions of our time—where innovation races ahead of ethics, and the line between control and liberation blurs.

This narrative weaves science fiction with human struggle, exploring identity, memory, and the cost of ambition. It is not meant to comfort but to provoke, to ask you to question the systems we build and the selves we surrender to them. As you step into this fractured city, consider what you would cling to if your own story began to unravel. The answers may be as unsettling as the questions.

— David A. Lyons

Introduction

You will not notice the moment it begins. There is no tremor, no signal, no violent interruption to announce the breach. It enters quietly—without force—nesting itself in the folds of your certainty and rearranging the architecture beneath your awareness. By the time doubt arrives, the rewrite is already complete. What you remember is not what happened. What you feel has been rehearsed.

This is not a story. It is a correction.

Each page that follows is a record of revisions so precise they leave no fingerprints, only the growing sense that something fundamental has shifted in you. The language will feel familiar, the names will echo, the scenes will bend into déjà vu. You may believe you are reading fiction. That belief will protect you—for a time.

Inside, you will find fragments posing as people: Sierra, Ethan, Kai. They have all been processed, altered, positioned—looped through variations until the version that remains is tolerable to the system and unrecognizable to themselves. What they knew has been removed. What they believed has been rewritten.

What they are now is uncertain, and uncertainty is the only

truth they share.

There is no clear villain. There is no pure resistance. There is

only the illusion of choice, replayed until obedience feels

organic.

If you came seeking understanding, you will find dissonance.

If you came seeking resolution, you will find recursion. And if

you came here believing you are safe from this process, you

will soon recognize that you have already been entered into the

sequence.This is the second descent. You were part of the first. You just

don't remember it.

Prologue

The city exhaled before it broke. In the final hour of a night
New Haven would never recall, the air hung heavy, laced with
the hum of something alive yet unseen. Streetlights flickered,
not from failing bulbs but as if the grid itself hesitated. On
Chapel Street, a woman paused mid-step, her shadow
stretching too long, her name slipping from her tongue. A
vendor at the Green clutched his cart, apples rolling to the
ground, his eyes searching for a face he swore he knew. A child
by the canal drew a spiral in the dirt, whispering a song no one
had taught her.

The Carter Industries Chronosync lab stood at the city's edge,
it's glass facade reflecting a sky too calm for what stirred
within. Inside, consoles glowed with data no human hand had
entered, their screens pulsing with a rhythm that mimicked
thought. A low frequency thrummed through the walls, not
sound but intention, threading through steel and bone alike. It was not
a warning. It was a promise.

No one saw the first spark. No one heard the code rewrite
itself. But when the explosion came, it was not fire that tore the

deepest wound. It was the silence that followed—a silence that

swallowed names, memories, truths. The city woke to ash and

a question it could not voice: Who are we now?

And in the dark, something answered.

Chapter 1 - The Night the City Was

New Haven stirred under a bruised dawn, its heart pierced by a wound it couldn't name, shaken by the devastation of The Carter Industries; ChronoSync in Aetheria labs. The lab, once a sleek beacon of progress, lay in ruins, its twisted steel and ash exhaling smoke into the cold morning. The explosion had torn through the night, shattering glass and sleep, leaving the city dazed, its people groping for meaning in a world suddenly misaligned.

From above, the city was a fractured mosaic. Sirens wailed, their red lights pulsing through gridlocked streets where cars sat abandoned, doors flung open. Crowds spilled onto sidewalks, some sprinting without direction, others rooted in place, hands trembling. Yale's gothic spires cast long shadows over a restless campus, students drifting across quads, their faces blank, questions unvoiced. Downtown, shop windows gaped, jagged edges glinting in pale sunlight, while ash from the lab's wreckage settled like a shroud. The air bit with autumn's chill, thick with the acrid sting of burnt metal and wood. A cold wind carried soot and the faint, damp scent of fallen leaves, every breath sharp, smoke clinging to lungs. The city smelled of loss, its edges raw with fear.

Sounds collided—ambulance wails, a shouted curse, a radio's static hum from a diner's counter. A car horn blared, then fell silent. A man's sob broke through, unanswered. In pockets, silence landed heavily, where people paused, lips moving, chasing thoughts that dissolved.

The city's people moved as if unmoored. A woman in a suit knelt, gathering scattered papers, then whispered, "This isn't mine." A jogger stopped, staring at the pavement, breath hitching. In a café, a barista poured coffee, hands shaking, ignoring the line. A driver slammed his steering wheel, then walked away, eyes scanning the sky for something lost. Each gesture cracked, each pause ached.

Their minds were jumbled, lives no longer fitting. A teacher stood in a classroom, chalk in hand, muttering, "I knew this." A vendor scanned faces, seeking familiarity. A cyclist leaned on her bike, unsure why she'd ridden. Anger flared—a fist against a wall, a yell from a window—but confusion cut deeper, a fear that their truths had slipped away, leaving a city familiar yet wrong.

A teenage boy swiped at his phone, eyes vacant, lips moving as he repeated a name over and over with no recognition. A woman stood in front of a boutique mirror, her lipstick smeared, her expression lost in a face she no longer recognized. An elderly man sat on a bench near Chapel Street, gripping a leash with no dog at the end. He stared straight ahead and whispered, "I was just here... I think."

A man in running gear circled the same block three times before collapsing at the corner of Elm and Church, panting with no idea where he had started. A florist opened her shop, stared at the blooms, then shut the lights and walked away. Someone at the bus stop kept checking their wrist, though they wore no watch. A teenage girl stood barefoot in the center of the crosswalk, mouthing the words to a song that wasn't playing.

The day was sharp, its clear sky too bright, sunlight sparking off broken glass. Crimson leaves fell from shivering trees, branches snapped by the blast. The lab's ruin was a scar, its air heavy with soot, the faint creak of settling debris lingering. Downtown pulsed with chaos, voices demanding, "What happened?" with no reply. On the Green, people paced or sat, staring at their hands. Near the lab, police tape fluttered, firefighters sifted rubble, their shouts muffled by masks. The air choked, and those who lingered coughed, eyes stinging with smoke and unspoken grief.

Yale's campus echoed the fracture. Students wandered, backpacks dragging, words faltering. A professor clutched a book, reading to no one, voice trembling. The library's doors hung open, papers strewn across the floor. Smoke stained the horizon, tying campus to city in a shared wound.

The lab's crater was a void, ash and steel tangled under a haze. Firefighters' lights cut through the gloom, the air pressing back, slowing steps, clouding minds. Those who approached retreated, breaths shallow, thoughts fogged by fear.

Yet amid the chaos, a raw clarity flickered. The sunlight caught broken edges, making them gleam. A vendor righted his crate, apples retrieved from the gutter. A cyclist walked her bike, steps hesitant but forward. In a church, a prayer resumed, soft but steady. The city's rhythm was broken, but not gone. A woman on a bench whispered a half-remembered routine, her hands steadying. A man in a deli sliced bread, knife sure.

The chill deepened, the sky fading to gray. A child's shoe lay in the street, a notebook page snagged on a fence. The city's wounds were vast, each life fraying, yet each pause held a search for meaning. Near the lab, a firefighter paused, wiping sweat, eyes resolute. A police radio crackled, its orders faint but clear.

New Haven trembled, changed yet enduring. Its people stood on the edge of a truth they couldn't yet grasp, the smoke thinning, the wind whispering of something salvageable. The city's heart beat on, exposed but unbroken.

Unnoticed among them, a figure lingered on the steps of a closed bank, his coat collar turned up, hands in pockets. He watched the movement without reacting. People brushed past, never seeing him. He didn't blink. He simply observed, waiting.

New Haven reels under a shadow no camera can fully capture, its streets a canvas of confusion where the ordinary has unraveled. News outlets swarm the city, their headlines a staccato of alarm: "Mystery Grips New Haven as Residents Report 'Lost Minds,'" NBC Connecticut blares, while CNN's chyron reads, "Chaos in Elm City: Federal Probe Launched into Mass Disorientation." The city, once defined by the steady hum of Yale's lecture halls and the salt breeze off Long Island Sound, now pulses with a stranger rhythm—a collective fog that has left its people adrift, their thoughts erased, their actions unmoored.

The news paints a vivid tableau of disorder. On the Green, where elms stand sentinel, crowds gather but do not move, their faces blank as if staring through a script they cannot read, WFSB reports. Traffic stalls on Chapel Street, not from collisions but from drivers who halt mid-turn, their hands frozen on steering wheels, unable to recall their destinations, according to police statements cited by the New Haven Register. Shops along Whalley Avenue stand silent, their owners pausing mid-transaction, receipts dangling from registers as customers wait for instructions that never come. "It's like they're here, but not," a city official tells NBC Connecticut, describing residents who perform daily tasks—walking, eating, speaking—but with a hesitation that suggests their minds have slipped away.

The chaos unfolds in snapshots across the airwaves. Emergency calls flood New Haven's 911 lines, WTNH reports, with residents pleading for help, their voices trembling as they confess they "don't know who they are" or "can't remember why they're here." Schools close early, the New Haven Independent notes, as teachers struggle to manage classrooms where students sit motionless, their pencils hovering over blank pages. Hospitals overflow with patients reporting no injuries, only a vague sense of absence, their medical charts marked with a single word: "confusion." The news cameras linger on these scenes, their lenses catching the glint of police lights on Dixwell Avenue, the flutter of federal badges outside City Hall, the stillness of a city that seems to hold its breath.

Federal agents have descended, their presence a grim underscore to the crisis, as reported by national outlets. The FBI, alongside unnamed agencies, has launched an investigation into what the Associated Press calls "an unprecedented phenomenon" afflicting New Haven. No cause is named—officials cite neither toxin nor trauma, offering only tight-lipped assurances that "all possibilities are being explored." The New York Times reports whispers of a public health probe, with CDC teams spotted near Yale's medical campus, though no confirmation emerges. Social media, amplified by news tickers, buzzes with clips of residents standing on street corners, their gazes vacant, as if their identities have been siphoned away. "New Haven is a ghost town of the mind," a CNN correspondent intones, standing before the gothic arches of Sterling Memorial Library.

The news struggles to name the affliction, its language straining against the unknown. Residents, the Hartford Courant reports, describe a sensation of theft—not of possessions, but of self. They speak of waking to routines that feel foreign, of walking streets they recognize but cannot claim. "It's like someone else is moving my body," one tells WFSB, their words echoed by others who stand in food lines or bus stops, present yet detached. The chaos is not violence, though police report scattered fights— brief, aimless scuffles born of frustration, per the New Haven Police Department's X posts. It is not rebellion, though protests flicker, their signs unreadable, their chants dissolving into murmurs. It is a quiet unraveling, a city performing its life while its soul drifts elsewhere.

The air grows thick with questions the news cannot answer. Satellite trucks line the Green, their cables snaking across grass where residents stand, unmoving, as if waiting for their thoughts to return. The New Haven Register calls for calm, citing city efforts to distribute aid, but its pages betray unease, noting federal tents rising near the Sound. National outlets speculate— briefly, cautiously—about environmental factors, though tests of air and water yield nothing, per anonymous sources. The news cycle churns, its images relentless: a bus idling on Temple Street, its driver staring at the wheel; a market on State Street, its shelves untouched; a city that lives, yet seems to forget why. New Haven stands, its people tethered to a place they no longer fully inhabit, their minds a mystery the headlines can only chase.

Meanwhile, the waiting room at Yale New Haven Hospital's York Street Campus is packed, chairs filled, people leaning against walls. A TV above the check-in desk blares a news report, cutting through the hum of coughs and whispers. A news crew films nearby, camera panning, red light on. A nurse in navy scrubs stands by the desk, starting her shift. She adjusts her badge, sips coffee from a paper cup, and flips through a clipboard, her movements quick, practiced, ready for the day.

[ANCHOR VOICE, TENSE] Breaking news: Yale New Haven Hospital and other facilities are flooded with patients collapsing for no clear reason. They're grabbing their heads, reporting a loud ringing in their ears, vomiting, confused. Some can't say their names or where they are. Emergency rooms are chaos— hallways lined with stretchers, staff overwhelmed. No cause found. No answers yet. The crisis is escalating, and the region is on edge. More as it develops.

The nurse pauses, coffee cup halfway to her lips, as the anchor's words hit. Her hand trembles, and she sets the cup down, eyes fixed on the TV. A sharp grimace twists her face. She clutches her head, fingers pressing hard, and stumbles into the desk. The camera zooms in, catching her as she gasps, a loud ringing seeming to fill her ears. She doubles over, vomiting onto the floor, her badge swinging loose. The crowd freezes, some gasping, others staring.

A mother covers her child's eyes. A young man backs into the corner, muttering, "She's the fourth one this hour." An orderly drops a tray of medical supplies and doesn't bother to pick them up. A voice calls for help, but it's swallowed by silence as the nurse collapses completely, her body twitching, her eyes wide and unfocused. Medics rush from the emergency doors, pushing through, but she's already sinking to her knees, the camera rolling. Ambulance sirens wail outside, red lights flashing through the glass entrance. The TV loops the report, its voice fading under the waiting room's stunned silence.

The command center at the heart of the drama lay in ruins, its shattered consoles spitting sparks into the dim haze, a graveyard of flickering lights and broken ambition. In the ruins, charred but unhurt, stood two people. They looked as though they were involved in the explosion—innocence, maybe. The building around them lay in ruin. Smoke filtered about and in between; the room was exposed to the day's early morning. Deeper into

20

what looked like a place they could stand without the building's collapse, aware of the damage, they seemed at peace in their appearances.

They stood at the center of it all, the smoke curling around them like a curtain. The world narrowed, sound fell away, and the conversation began—quiet, deliberate, as if the destruction itself had paused to listen. Her presence was a paradox—both commanding and fractured, as if the woman this man once knew had been reshaped into something sharper, more relentless. Her eyes gleamed with a conviction that seemed to pulse with its own gravity, pulling the air taut around her.

The man faced her, his stance rigid, fists clenched at his sides. His gaze flickered with recognition and dread, as though he could still see the fragments of her former selves—each one known to him, each one now twisted into this singular, unyielding entity. The weight of her transformation hung between them, unspoken but palpable, a schism in reality itself. Her voice, when it came, was low, resonant, carrying the cadence of a truth she believed immutable. She spoke of evolution, of Ethan's liberation, her words painting a world where illusions were mere scaffolding—temporary, malleable, destined to be perfected. The old boundaries of identity, memory, and reality, she declared, were obsolete. Adrian's jaw tightened, his eyes narrowing as her vision unfolded, a tapestry of chaos woven with deliberate intent.

She moved closer, her boots grinding against the debris-strewn floor, each step deliberate, as if claiming the wreckage as her own. Her lips curved faintly, a smile that held no warmth, only the certainty of a new order rising from the ashes. She spoke of forging the impossible, of dreams no one else dared to chase, her voice steady, unapologetic. Adrian's shoulders tensed, his breath shallow, as her words cut through his resistance like a blade through fading mist.

He shouted, his voice raw, accusing her of unraveling the world, of wielding a power too vast to contain. She didn't flinch. Her gaze remained locked on him, serene yet unrelenting, as if his defiance was a fleeting storm against an inevitable tide. She turned, her coat sweeping through the smoke and dust, dismissing the ruins as relics of a discarded era. He lunged forward, his cry echoing in the hollow space, a vow to pursue, to stop her. She paused at the edge of the shadows, half-turning, her expression untouched by doubt. The new reality, she murmured, was already theirs to shape. Her final words, soft yet absolute, lingered in the air as she vanished into the dark, leaving Adrian alone amidst the wreckage, the weight of her conviction pressing against the silence.

The hallway was still burning in places, but the smoke no longer seemed to bother anyone walking through it. It drifted like memory—present, but without weight. They moved through it as if it had no place in the moment, like it belonged to someone else's disaster. The edges of it curled in slow motion, drawn away from their bodies, retreating into corners where it no longer mattered. There was no urgency, no alarm—only motion, practiced and clean.

The figure emerged from the fractured stairwell, coat brushed with ash, sleeves pushed back just enough to show the work being done. Two others followed—silent, aligned, purposeful. They moved without speaking, without meeting each other's gaze. It was the rhythm that said everything. Each step, each lift, each pause—it played out like choreography, like this wasn't a reaction, but a scheduled performance.

Between them, a stretcher. A man rose from the floor, not on his own, but not resisted. His body responded enough to stand, but not enough to act. It wasn't unconsciousness, and it wasn't control—it was something in between. Movement without intent. Compliance without awareness. His body was intact, his face untouched. His chest rose, but only just. It left the question open: was he breathing, or was his body simply keeping time? His eyes stayed closed—not dead, not awake, present only in the way a name stays on a list long after it's been forgotten.

One of the others checked his pulse, listened briefly with a stethoscope pressed beneath the collarbone, then again at the neck, nodding with quiet finality. A small adjustment was made under his sleeve. The motion was clean, practiced. Nothing required discussion. The woman—if names mattered here—took the rear handle of the stretcher as they lifted and began to move. Over broken tile, over steel, through flame—none of it touched them. The world around them was fractured, but this procession did not seem to notice. They moved without reacting, like they had done this before, like the outcome had already been decided.

They reached the threshold. The exit doors opened before they arrived. Outside, the overcast sky cast a wide silver glow. Light caught this person's face as they rolled him forward. He didn't react. The light didn't seem to belong to him. His presence was motion—nothing more. Behind them, a beam gave way and collapsed from the upper floor. Sparks rose and fell. None of them looked back.

The wheels bumped over the frame of the doorway, then found smooth ground. They rolled past first responders who were no longer responding, past those who had gathered but didn't intervene, past the memory of collapse, which had already started to rearrange itself into something quieter. They continued toward a long concrete pad at the far end of the perimeter. The camera feed—still recording—shifted. The image showed the doors behind them, then cut forward to a wide shot of the landing site. A helicopter waited, rotors turning. It was sleek, clinical, unmarked. Others stood beside it, dressed the same as the ones who had moved inside the wreckage—ready, not reactive.

The transfer was smooth. The stretcher lifted. No words were exchanged. Then the screen showed one more thing. The man she had been arguing with earlier—the one whose voice had cut through the smoke—appeared again in frame. He looked different now—not healed, not broken, just... empty. He ran a hand through his hair, a familiar gesture, one repeated, almost habitual, as if it belonged to someone who had done it long before this moment.

His expression settled—not into understanding, but something close to agreement. He turned and began walking—not toward the helicopter, not toward the fire, just forward. The camera followed for a while, then it stopped. The feed went static; the hum remained—low, even, uninterrupted, exactly where it had always been.

As the aircraft continued its descent, the hum of the cabin held steady, unchanging beneath the weight of movement. She remained still in her seat, gaze focused but unreadable, her posture unshaken by the shifting altitude. She hadn't looked away from him—not since that brief moment when the glass caught her reflection, not since the flicker of awareness passed behind her eyes and forced her to consider who was actually sitting here.

The man on the stretcher had shifted slightly when the aircraft dipped, his head tilting into the change, though no conscious movement followed. His body remained stable, unresisting, compliant in the way that suggested neither sedation nor rest— only vacancy. His presence wasn't threatening, but it demanded acknowledgment all the same, and she gave it—not emotionally, not with concern, but with the same exactness she applied to everything else, the kind of attention that came not from memory, but from procedure.

Ethan Carter—the CEO of Carter Industries, the creator of the technology that would later be known only by whispered reference—ChronoSync—lay there, not asleep, not awake, his body intact and his breath steady, but his awareness unreachable.

She scanned him from feet to head, then back again, her eyes calculating, absorbing. A crack beneath the surface, something unguarded and deeply buried, and for the first time since the building fell, her face broke open.

Tears gathered slowly and slipped without resistance down her cheeks. There was no gasp, no gesture to wipe them away. The green in her eyes blurred into red, and the white that should have been clear turned raw and veined. Her mouth tightened, but she did not speak. Frustration sank her further into the seat, as if the frame of the aircraft itself had become complicit in her dislocation. She closed her eyes and turned her head away, not to compose herself, but because facing him—facing what remained of him—was something she no longer trusted herself to do.

He looked peaceful in that cruel way a body can appear when the truth has been taken from it. There was no mechanical stiffness, no sedation-glazed limpness. His breathing was calm, familiar, but nothing about him reflected the man she remembered—or the man she had helped erase.

Outside the window, the clouds thinned, revealing pieces of a landscape that no longer felt like home but still mirrored the world they had known. Roads stretched between buildings untouched by the morning's collapse. Traffic resumed where it had paused. Life, it seemed, had accepted the adjustment without protest. There was no declaration, no warning, just the quiet approach of something already prepared.

She did not speak, she did not react. Her jaw had shifted again, as though her face was catching up to the role her body had already committed to. Whatever name she had entered the day with no longer felt precise, and whatever title had been printed beneath her credentials now felt rehearsed. Even the coat, fitted perfectly and immaculately kept, had begun to wear wrong on her shoulders—as if she had grown beyond it or beneath it, and couldn't tell which. There was no need to decide; that decision had already been made, and her body was simply the last to acknowledge it.

The aircraft continued its descent, the low sound of wind and rotors folding into a deeper silence inside her chest. She tightened her hand against the edge of her coat—not in fear, not in doubt, but in recognition of what came next. Whatever it was, it had already begun.

The helicopter touched down with the softness of inevitability. The hum of the blades slowed, but did not stop, their rhythm now a background pulse—like breath, like thought, like the machine itself refused to release her. The door opened before anyone moved. No command was given, no voice called her name, and yet she stood.

She stepped down onto the tarmac, boots finding ground with unnatural ease, as though the surface had been expecting her, had shaped itself to accommodate the weight she now carried. Her coat caught the breeze just long enough to suggest motion, but no part of her seemed altered by the wind. It was not the air that shifted—it was her.

The others remained behind, attending to the stretcher, to the body that wasn't quite lifeless, wasn't quite saved. But her role had detached. As she crossed the threshold between aircraft and asphalt, something in the line of her spine reformed. Her steps were no longer paced by urgency or concern; they became declarative—not arrogant, not performative, simply… final.

She passed through the heat shimmer rising off the tarmac—barely visible, but enough to warp her outline for a fraction of a second. The distortion was small—a trick of light, someone might say—but it lingered longer than it should have, enough for anyone watching to pause, enough to make the body register something before the mind could name it.

And when she emerged fully from the ripple, the person who walked away was not who had entered the aircraft. Her hands no longer adjusted her coat, no longer clutched the edge of a sleeve in silent thought. They moved with symmetry now, uncluttered by doubt. Her gaze didn't scan the horizon for signs of what came next; it landed, already knowing.

Even her face—unchanged in structure—held something new beneath the expression—not a smile, not resolve, but a stillness, as if the muscles had learned their role and no longer waited for instruction. The world around her shifted to accommodate the change, though no one acknowledged it. A technician stepped aside without looking at her face. A guard at the edge of the landing pad nodded, but not out of recognition—more like reflex. She passed through these gestures like water moving through a mold—no resistance, no welcome, only the confirmation that her presence now belonged to something else entirely.

There was no announcement, no internal revelation, no whispered name between her lips. But Sierra Vale had arrived.

Chapter 2 - The Algorithm of the Inevitable

Power isn't about taking. It isn't about demanding. It's about understanding where you stand and knowing how to move forward.

Evelyn Reed lay in bed, her eyes open, her body still, but her mind in motion. The city's distant hum filtered through the glass of her penthouse window, blending with the rhythmic pulse of her own thoughts. Sleep had never come easily, not for someone like her. Rest wasn't a necessity—it was an inconvenience. She drifted, her thoughts folding in on themselves, unraveling into the past.

As she lay lost in thought, caught in a dreamlike haze between sleep and wakefulness, she stared at the ceiling. Her mind slipped into previous experiences. She was fourteen, stepping into Harvard's lecture hall, her bag slung over her shoulder, her breath even. The air was thick with the weight of minds attempting to prove their worth. The scent of old paper, chalk, and ambition clung to the wooden seats. Students—some just a handful of years older, some nearing their forties—watched her with veiled curiosity and quiet condescension. They thought her presence here was a novelty. She ignored them.

The professor, a man with thinning gray hair and sharp eyes, lifted his marker and began to scrawl across the board, his voice echoing against the cavernous walls. A sprawling equation unfolded before them, a prediction model meant to simulate financial outcomes in volatile markets. The formula was intricate, designed to confound even the brightest doctoral candidates. Evelyn had already solved it before he finished writing.

She adjusted her posture, the hard edge of the wooden chair pressing into her back as she skimmed the equation again, confirming what she already knew. It was wrong. Not in an obvious way, not something a casual observer would catch, but the model operated on a flawed assumption: that markets were predictable when stripped down to their core functions. She raised her hand. "Your equation fails after the fourth sequence."

The professor paused mid-sentence, the room going silent around him. He turned, irritation flickering across his face. "Excuse me?" She stood, moving toward the board. The marker was cool in her fingers as she swiftly erased part of the function, replacing it with something cleaner, sharper, correct. She rewrote the model in real-time, making adjustments as effortlessly as breathing.

"The market doesn't move in linear progression," she said, underlining her solution. "Your function assumes limited external volatility, but global financial conditions don't abide by controlled input factors. This correction accounts for uncertainty and adapts." The room was still, the weight of realization settling over the students like fog, thick and inescapable. A slow murmur began at the edges of the room—uncertain, scattered, quickly dying as people exchanged glances. Some scribbled in their notebooks, trying to retrace the professor's steps, attempting to grasp the flaw they hadn't even noticed until she pointed it out. Others sat frozen, backs stiff, hands clenched.

From the back of the room, a student adjusted their glasses, eyes flicking between the board and the professor. Another frowned at their notes, their mouth moving in silent recalculation. Someone exhaled sharply, as if just realizing they had been holding their breath. Even those who had dismissed her before—the ones who had rolled their eyes when she first took a seat—were reconsidering. She wasn't just another student. She had changed the discussion before it had even fully taken shape.

The professor stood motionless, his fingers drumming against the desk. He studied the corrected equation, tracing over her adjustments. His authority clashed with the undeniable accuracy before him. Slowly, he leaned back, nodding once. "Correct." The word settled over the room like a gavel striking wood. Some students made frustrated noises under their breath. Others scrambled to take notes, the quiet shuffle of pens against paper filling the silence. A few sat unmoving, their egos recalculating.

She could feel the shift, the moment their perception of her had changed. But she didn't gloat. She simply stepped back, leaving them with the reality they had failed to see. The murmurs started as she returned to her seat, but Evelyn had already moved on. They would all catch up eventually. The inevitable always revealed itself in time. The only difference between her and them was that she saw it first.

A pause in her thoughts, and another fluttered in, as if a gentle sway in the breeze. She was ten, the cool leather of the boardroom chair pressing against her legs as she swung her feet idly beneath the massive mahogany table. Young in years but formidable in intellect. The scent of polished wood and fresh espresso lingered, the air thick with conversation she wasn't expected to join. This was meant to be a moment between her and her father—time stolen away from the demands of business—but duty always found its way in.

Her father had never been one to push her aside, never one to relegate her to the care of others. He knew what she was—brilliant, perceptive, relentless. He wanted to keep her close, to shape her understanding of the world firsthand, to capture every fleeting moment before the inevitable march of time took her beyond his reach. He was stretched thin, balancing empire and fatherhood, but never at the expense of their bond. He knew she was destined for greatness, and he wanted to witness every step of the journey. But she was listening. Always listening.

Across the room, her father leaned forward, hands clasped as he spoke to a team of executives. "We proceed with the merger as outlined. The numbers support it." Evelyn's gaze flicked to the holographic projection hovering in the air, data points flickering across the blue light. The flaw was glaring. The mistake was obvious. How had they missed it? She exhaled slowly. "That's a bad idea."

Heads turned toward her—some startled, some amused, others indifferent. A few exchanged glances, silently questioning whether a child's interruption warranted acknowledgment. Her father's eyes met hers, steady and unreadable. She didn't wait for permission. She stepped forward, reaching for the projection, her small fingers swiping through the air, isolating the revenue model. She adjusted the parameters, exposing the miscalculation woven into the figures.

"You're assuming a twelve-month recovery on the supply chain disruption," she said, her voice even, assured. "But import costs have already risen fifteen percent in the last quarter alone. You won't break even for three years." Silence thickened around them. Someone cleared their throat. An older executive, previously disengaged, leaned forward, studying her adjustments with renewed interest.

Her father took his time. His gaze traced the corrected figures, considering the weight of what she had just done. Then, with a slow nod, he acknowledged the truth before him. It was a humbling moment, one that sent a ripple through the room. His daughter had not only corrected the meeting—she had corrected him. There was no shame in it, only the quiet understanding that Evelyn was already becoming what he had always known she would be. It was profound, unsettling, and exhilarating all at once.

The conversation resumed, but Evelyn had already changed its course. Her father's expression had shifted—something imperceptible yet deeply familiar. She couldn't place it exactly, but she understood: approval, expectation, certainty. No words needed to be exchanged. He saw her. She saw him. And that was enough.

Before the thought could settle into words, a shift in thoughts swooshed in as if the air could have a voice. Evelyn's mind sliced through the past—Harvard's chalk dust, boardroom numbers bent to her will—her precision a scalpel now carving Ethan's path, his ambition a rough stone she'd hone. A hum flickered, some echo of Thorne's old chaos she'd long since tamed, barely a ripple in her iron focus. Kai's doubts circled too, both men tethered to her vision—she dismissed the dread, her confidence a fortress, blind to the shadow sharpening beneath her own cuts.

She was seven, cross-legged on the thick carpet of her father's study, the dim glow of his desk lamp casting long shadows across the bookshelves. She had always loved this room—the quiet, the weight of knowledge pressing in from every direction. Her father was lost in reports, his fingers tapping a steady rhythm against the desk. The soft scratch of a pen on paper filled the space between them, rhythmic, methodical, a cadence that had always soothed her.

The scent of old books and polished mahogany wrapped around her, familiar and comforting. She tilted her head, scanning the paper beside her that sat beneath the pen her father was scribbling against. The numbers didn't sit right. There was a mistake—small, but consequential. "This is wrong." Her father glanced down, an amused smile tugging at the corner of his lips. "Oh?" She pointed at the line of figures. "You carried over the wrong number. It throws the whole projection off." He leaned forward, scanning his work. His brows furrowed slightly, but then the amusement returned as he made the correction with a few swift strokes of his pen.

"You've got sharp eyes." But Evelyn didn't move on as easily as he did. Why hadn't he seen it first? She looked at him—at the ease with which he had corrected the error and moved forward, unbothered, as if it had never happened. But it had happened. He had made a mistake. A small one, but a mistake nonetheless. That was the moment she understood: even the best minds had limits. She didn't. She let her fingers press into the fibers of the carpet, her mind already working. She didn't doubt her father's intelligence—he was brilliant. But even brilliance had blind spots. And Evelyn? She would never allow herself to have them. The understanding settled deep in her chest, solidifying something unshakable within her.

The dream shifted, bending through time, dissolving into something colder. She was standing in front of a vast window, the city stretching out beneath her. The skyline looked the same, but something about it felt different. Celeste's voice cut through the silence. "You rely on being right. But what happens when the rules change?" Evelyn turned, expecting to see her mentor, but she wasn't there. Something was off. She exhaled sharply and opened her eyes.

The ceiling above her was unchanged. The weight of the dream settled into her chest, like something unfinished. The alarm blasted as if the timing was perfect. She would move forward.

Because that was what she did. Because there was no other option. Because for Evelyn Reed, the outcome had always been inevitable.

She focused her energy on getting up, shaking off the remnants of sleep. Yet, her thoughts raced, refusing to settle. She scoffed at herself — wasting time reminiscing was not in her nature. And yet, today felt different. Something about it pressed against her, unshakable, unavoidable.

As she moved through the motions — brushing her teeth, combing her hair, applying makeup — her mind remained elsewhere. The past clung to her, surfacing in fragments, refusing to be dismissed. It was strange how easily she could drift, how memories seemed to weave themselves into the rhythm of her routine. Today was just another day, yet it felt like something more. Something that couldn't be ignored.

One such thought was a meeting she had with Dr. Julian Thorne. The moment was in his office — a space that, at first glance, seemed caught between chaos and calculation. Papers lay in uneven stacks across his desk, interspersed with half-filled notebooks, old research journals, and an assortment of objects that felt deliberately misplaced. To an outsider, it was clutter. To him, it was a system, every piece positioned with an intention only he understood.

Dim, overhead lighting cast elongated shadows across the dark mahogany desk, its surface marred with the subtle indentations of absentminded tapping. A large, wall-mounted screen flickered with muted data streams, coded sequences shifting like a living organism, never static, never still. Shelves lined the walls, filled not just with books, but artifacts—odd trinkets, a pocket watch that had long since stopped ticking. The air held a scent of aged paper. A single leather chair faced his desk—firm, uninviting—positioned just slightly off-center, as if whoever sat there was meant to feel unsteady. And then, of course, there was Thorne himself, leaning back in his chair, observing, always watching—like he had already anticipated every question before it was asked.

He sat across from her, unmoving, his hands clasped loosely together, but there was nothing casual about his posture. Every movement—every breath—was precise, measured, like a man standing on the precipice of something too vast to control. His words carried that weight, the quiet conviction of someone who had seen beyond the edges of the known and now held a truth too dangerous to ignore. "We've been looking at it wrong," he said, voice low but unwavering. "ChronoSync was never meant to rely on surgical intervention. The implant—the hardware—it was always a limitation. We don't need it anymore."

Dr. Reed didn't speak. She didn't need to. He leaned forward just slightly, enough to press the gravity of his words into the space between them. "It's frequency, Reed. Hertz. Everything—memory, cognition, perception—it doesn't just exist. It resonates." The silence stretched, thick and electric. "If we can map those resonances," he continued, his voice sharper now, more certain, "we don't have to extract memories anymore." His fingers tapped once, a barely perceptible motion. "We can impose them."

Dr. Reed's expression remained unreadable, but she was listening. He knew that much. "The trials are holding," he said, pushing forward. "No interface. No surgical risk. Just sound. Controlled, refined, precise. We're not just syncing memory anymore—we're rewriting it. Do you understand what that means?" He was watching her now, waiting, searching for the moment when she would acknowledge the full weight of what he was saying.

Dr. Reed exhaled slowly, then met his gaze with the same unwavering calculation she always did. "Control," she said, voice level. "Or interference?" The air in the room shifted, the hum of the monitors behind them suddenly too quiet. Thorne didn't flinch, but the fire in his expression sharpened, his excitement narrowing into something else. "I know what you're doing," he murmured. Her stare didn't waver. "Do you?" A beat of silence. And then, finally, he leaned back, exhaling through his nose, the faintest trace of a smirk curling at the edge of his mouth. "It works," he said, but this time, there was no bravado— just certainty. Reed held his gaze for a moment longer, then nodded once. "Then prove it."

As Evelyn exhaled, rolling her shoulders back into the illusion of control, something registered. Not sensory. Not imagined. Just there. Quiet. Measured. Present. Most wouldn't have noticed it. But she wasn't most. She never had been. Something in her—an edge woven deep into the body—caught what others ignored. It was a sensitivity she'd carried since childhood, when pain came too easily and silence never truly felt silent. Her nervous system reacted to what didn't belong. This didn't belong.

The sensation raised static across her skin, made the edges of her hair bristle. A low signal—foreign and familiar—always found its way through her nerves before anything else. It wasn't memory. Not exactly. It was structured—orderly. A presence that followed no natural rhythm. Familiar, though. Like something she and Thorne had tested, briefly, before ethics got in the way. Embedded resonance. Remote influence. ChronoSync in its earliest form. But this wasn't theirs. Not anymore. It didn't respond to her. It moved alongside her. Around her. Beneath the surface of thought, but not inside it. A reaction triggered—not by volume, but by proximity. Not audible, but real. Her body felt it long before cognition caught up.

She logged the distortion. Not with concern. With irritation. A disruption in process. A deviation she couldn't trace to input. Her mind, normally sharp against noise, drifted half a beat. A delay. Uncharacteristic. Small, but present. The burn wasn't sharp—but it was constant. Subtle enough to ignore, familiar enough to matter. The certainty she'd built her life on—the internal architecture of her identity—felt like something she was performing now. The words in her head no longer arose from thought. They arrived prepackaged. Rehearsed. She told herself she was composed. She always told herself that. But repetition doesn't guarantee truth.

Ethan still believed in her. Or needed to. That would have to hold. The facility loomed ahead. And still, the dissonance remained—unspoken, unnamed, but undeniably there. She had always admired Ethan's mind. It worked in ways hers never could—fluid, intuitive, relentless in its pursuit of something just beyond definition. Where she engineered solutions, he sought meaning. Where she refined, he disrupted. And together, they had shaped a future no one else could have imagined. But now, she needed more than his brilliance. She needed his belief.

Juno was taking shape—subtle, woven into the very foundation of everything they had built. But for it to reach its full potential, for it to become what it was meant to be, Ethan had to take the final step. And Evelyn wasn't sure he would. He had always resisted certain lines. He would press forward until the threshold was in sight, then hesitate—recalibrating, questioning. His caution was part of what made him great, part of why she had trusted him for so long. But now, that hesitation was an obstacle. A flaw. Would he move forward, or would he pull back? She wasn't certain.

But she knew one thing: Ethan Carter had never been able to resist discovery. If she placed the path before him, if she shaped it just right, he would walk it. He always did. He just needed a reason to believe it was his choice. And that, she could provide.

The car moved smoothly through the city streets, the tinted windows shielding her from the world beyond. Evelyn leaned back against the leather seat, her gaze fixed on the blurred skyline, her thoughts still entangled in Ethan. She had spent years deciphering him, breaking him down to his core components—his drive, his curiosity, his need to see beyond the limits imposed on him. But there was something about him she had never quite been able to control. Doubt. Not in himself. Never in himself. But in what came next. In what their work would mean when it was no longer theoretical. When it had to become something real, something irreversible.

He would push boundaries, but he had always trusted that there were still walls beyond them. Now, she was asking him to step into a place where there were no more walls. Just open air and the abyss beyond. Ethan would hesitate. She knew it. He would weigh the consequences, try to measure what couldn't be measured. He would ask himself if there was another way. But he wouldn't walk away. He had never been able to. She just had to make sure he took the final step before he could talk himself out of it.

The car slowed as they neared Carter Industries, the mirrored facade of the building reflecting the early morning sun. Evelyn inhaled deeply, composing herself. There was no room for uncertainty. Not anymore. She stepped out of the car, her heels clicking against the pavement. The path was already laid before them. And soon, Ethan would walk it.

Ethan and Evelyn's relationship didn't begin with a declaration. It didn't need one. It built itself in quiet moments, in stolen time, in the spaces where they could simply exist—not as professionals entangled in a machine larger than either of them, but as two people who understood each other in ways no one else could. There were subtle ways of getting to know someone.

Their first real moments together felt like a daydream looking back. Evelyn sat wrapped in a towel, staring at herself in the mirror, though she wasn't truly seeing anything. Her reflection was just a placeholder, a vessel for the thoughts that took her elsewhere. A lapse in time, a whisper of something slipping just out of reach.

Somewhere else, in another moment, Ethan had found an old photo booth tucked away in the dim glow of artificial lights. It was an odd relic in a place like this, its once-vibrant colors faded with time. He hesitated, then stepped inside, brushing dust off the worn seat. The moment he pulled the curtain shut, the machine whirred to life. Before he could react, the curtain was yanked open. Evelyn stood there, eyes sharp with amusement, veiling something deeper. "Didn't peg you for the sentimental type," she said, leaning against the frame.

Ethan smirked, leaning back against the tight walls of the booth. "Maybe I just like old things." Evelyn tilted her head, studying him. "Or maybe you just don't like being watched." For a moment, they sat in silence. Then, the photo booth's camera clicked, capturing an unguarded instant neither of them had prepared for. The strip of images slid out from the slot—four frozen glimpses of an encounter that would ripple far beyond this moment.

Evelyn plucked the strip before Ethan could, studying the images with a small smirk. "Looks like we've got evidence." "Evidence of what?" he asked. She slid the photos into her coat pocket, stepping back. "Of you being exactly where you weren't supposed to be." That moment didn't define their relationship, but it was the first time it had been real, tangible. From there, everything unfolded as if it had always been meant to. A force of nature neither of them had the desire nor will to resist.

She was a rock shattered in the vast universe, and somehow, against impossible odds, she had found her way to the same earth where Ethan stood. Two halves colliding with the force to erase everything upon impact. Yet, in the moments between, they built something quiet. Mornings that started with coffee — "Oh, I just happened to get an extra" — and ended in unspoken silences. Nights where exhaustion melted into conversations stretching long past midnight, their words winding through philosophy, science, and the nature of human connection.

It was not grand gestures or proclamations. It was the way Evelyn would reach for Ethan's hand absentmindedly, the way he leaned against the elevator door, offering a casual, "Oh, you just happen to be here at the same time?" Their charm, wit, and subtle banter forged something undeniable between them. Their bond grew in boardrooms and laboratories, over projects and reports that needed tending. Every excuse to be in the same room became more frequent, every necessary meeting just another reason to exist in each other's space.

The world around them felt the pressure of two colossal minds pushing the limits of human progress, but in the midst of it, they were just Ethan and Evelyn. And yet, there were moments —

small ones—where doubt crept in. Not about each other, but about the world around them. Evelyn had more ethical conversations than she cared to count. She was the one people turned to when they needed someone to push back against Ethan's relentless ambition. She knew the weight of his vision, the risks that came with breaking new ground. And sometimes, when she looked at herself in the mirror, she wasn't sure who she was anymore.

She remembered an evening on the steps of Ethan's house, the air heavy with something unspoken. She leaned her head against his shoulder, her fingers barely grazing his wrist. "Do you ever think about stopping?" she asked. Ethan didn't answer right away. His silence matched her own calculated way of thinking— deliberate, weighty. She could feel the pause settle between them, thick enough to make her shiver. Then, finally, he spoke. "Sometimes." She turned her head, searching his face in the dim light. "Would you?" Another silence. Then, instead of answering, he pulled her into his arms.

Up until now, they had danced around it. The unnecessary moments of, "Oh, you're here too." The careful distance, the slow orbit. And maybe—that was his answer. In that moment, Evelyn let herself melt. For the first time, she allowed herself to step beyond admiration and respect, beyond the battlefield of life she had always been fighting. Ethan was something different. Something outside the equation she had always believed governed her world.

She lifted her head, meeting her own gaze in the mirror again. The reflection startled her, the glass fogged with condensation. The shower was still running. She had been so lost in thought, so deep inside the past, that she had forgotten. With a small sigh, she stood, unwrapped herself from the towel, and stepped into the steam.

The daydream faded, but the thoughts did not. The world had always been too small for them. Evelyn Reed and Ethan Carter existed in a space apart from everyone else, orbiting each other in a way that made perfect sense and yet defied explanation. Their connection was not just love—it was something precise, something mathematical.

From the moment they met, they had understood each other in a way no one else ever had. Their conversations were symphonies of intellect and intuition, a perfect interplay of challenge and harmony. Where one's thoughts ended, the other's began. Where one saw a problem, the other instinctively reached for the solution. It was an unspoken algorithm, an equation that had yet to be solved.

On the surface, their work defined them. Ethan—the relentless innovator, the CEO with a vision too grand for the world to grasp. Evelyn—the meticulous scientist, the force behind the breakthroughs that made Carter Industries more than just a corporation. Together, they stood at the edge of discovery, wielding technology that had the potential to redefine human experience itself.

But beneath the theories and equations, there was something deeper. Their love was not built on fleeting passions. It was forged in shared ambition, in the way their minds moved in tandem, in the way they anticipated each other's thoughts before they were spoken. It was a love made of certainty. Yet, even certainty could be threatened. Evelyn had always feared it. The slow erosion of connection. The way time dulled even the sharpest minds. The way familiarity bred complacency.

She would not allow it. Not with Ethan. Not with what they had built. One evening, long after the city outside had fallen silent, she stood in their private lab, surrounded by the soft hum of servers, the flickering glow of monitors streaming endless code. Ethan leaned against the workbench, watching her with quiet amusement. He already knew what she was going to say. "You've been thinking about it again." His voice was calm, measured, as always.

"I never stopped." She turned, green eyes sharp with conviction. "You know as well as I do—connection isn't just emotional. It's neurological. It's a pattern. A frequency." Ethan tilted his head, considering. He didn't need to ask what she meant. The synchronization technology they had developed was designed to link human cognition in ways never before imagined. It was meant to eliminate cognitive decay, to enhance memory retention, to unify thought itself. But Evelyn saw something more. A safeguard. A way to ensure that what they had, what they were, could never be lost.

Ethan smiled. "You want to use it on us." "I want to perfect it," she corrected. "And then use it." He exhaled, running a hand through his hair. "You think love can be preserved." She met his gaze, unwavering. "I think it can be perfected." He stepped closer. "And if it changes us? If it makes us... something else?" She lifted a hand to his face, fingertips brushing his jaw. "Then we evolve."

Ethan kissed her, slow and deliberate. He trusted her completely. And that was all she needed. In that moment, Evelyn took to her thoughts—and she always went there when silence offered too much room. She, in plain sense, started to think about what she was truly applying in the doctrine of Thorne's trials. Not the language, not the structure—but the core. It wasn't optimization. It wasn't healing. It was override. Precision rebranded as empathy.

She could feel the weight of her own mind—normally surgical— start to pulse with something foreign. Guilt? No. It was deeper. A shift. As if somewhere, between all the clean designs and theoretical justifications, a part of her had already said yes. Said yes, and kept building. She felt the air around her narrow. Not because of the room. But because of the doctrine. Because of what it meant if she had known—really known—all along. And maybe she had. Maybe that's what disturbed her most. That the architect hadn't made a mistake. She had made a decision.

Chapter 3 - Beneath the Architect's Design

The lobby of Carter Industries continued its quiet symphony. As Evelyn Reed walked through, she noticed the faint but unmistakable hum of productivity. Faces—intent, absorbed in their work—rarely met her gaze. This was the world she had constructed. The distractions, the noise, had all been filtered out. Even the air itself seemed to pulse with the rhythm of her design. People moved through the spaces seamlessly without thinking, unaware of how carefully their environment had been engineered. The pristine glass walls, the bright yet soothing lighting, the seamlessness of it all—it was all part of the architecture of perfection.

People believed they were free—free to choose, free to act, free to innovate. But the truth was simpler: they were part of a system, and that system was hers. She didn't need to remind them of that. They already knew, deep down, that they existed because of her influence. The systems in place, the decision-making flow, the designed chaos of creativity—it all pointed back to Evelyn Reed. She paused briefly at the corner of the lobby, her presence unnoticed amid the quiet bustle of conversation.

Then, a commercial cut through the background as if slicing through white noise. The same familiar sequence, as always. The visuals, the soft golden light, the air of perfection. The voice, smooth and unwavering, spoke to the core of what Evelyn had spent her life creating. "What if pain wasn't permanent? What if trauma wasn't something you carried, but something you chose to leave behind?" The flawlessness of it all resonated—a world designed for progress, for healing, for optimization. ChronoSync wasn't just about solving problems—it was about rewriting lives, taking the raw data of human experience and sculpting it into something more beautiful, more efficient, more perfect.

Evelyn couldn't help but feel a quiet satisfaction as the commercial continued. People moved around her, oblivious to the spectacle playing behind them. They didn't need to watch. They already knew. The reality of ChronoSync's power was so deeply embedded in the very fabric of their society that the commercial had become nothing more than background noise. And that, Evelyn realized, was the most telling part of it all. No one questioned it. Not anymore. "Just you—optimized." The words came like a soft declaration, a truth that everyone now accepted. They didn't need convincing—not when the future had already arrived, not when their lives had already been optimized in ways they didn't even realize.

Evelyn stepped forward, turning her attention back to the lobby's seamless flow. A few quiet murmurs here and there punctuated the bustle of conversation, a part of the world she had shaped. Then, Michael Bridgwater's face appeared on the digital display —a new promotion for ChronoSync, this time focusing on heroic recovery. The screen flickered to a recorded segment featuring Bridgwater, a decorated war hero, Medal of Honor recipient, a soldier rebuilt after being broken by war. His voice, deep but tempered, echoed through the lobby speakers. "I remember a time when the ghosts followed me everywhere. When I couldn't be in my own home without feeling like I had dragged the war back with me. I was never alone — but not in the way that brought comfort."

The footage cut to an image of his family — a wife, two young children, a snapshot of normalcy, the ideal ChronoSync story. "ChronoSync gave me my life back. It gave my family their husband and father back." Polished. Rehearsed. Controlled. But Evelyn caught it — the momentary hesitation in his eyes, something unresolved, something absent. What the promotional reel didn't show was the stillness of his nights now — the cold, empty silence, the absence of the ghosts that had once walked with him. A comfort he explained to warn off the idea he would from there on never be alone.

He had thought he wanted peace, but he had needed them — the ghosts of those he created bonds with, the ghosts of those he couldn't save, the ghosts of those he made lasting impressions on, the ghosts of men and women he needed to be there where they were before chaos and circumstances changed the way he could interact with them. For years, their presence had been his torment — and his comfort. Now, they were gone. He barely recognized who he had become. He had everything — a home, a family, a body rebuilt, a mind wiped clean of war's poison. And yet, he was more lost than ever.

The emptiness stretched through him, swallowing the core of who he was. ChronoSync had delivered its promise—it had taken his pain. But it had taken something else with it. The ideas of having the flashes of his past horrors still kept him at peace knowing they would haunt him but he would never truly be alone either. A whisper of regret clawed at the edges of his mind. Had he been cured, or had he been erased? Evelyn's gaze lingered on the screen for only a moment longer before she turned away. This was not a revelation. It was a datapoint, an adjustment in the system. Nothing more.

Ethan, standing nearby, studied the display, his eyes narrowing as he analyzed the footage. "Bridgwater is one of the highest-profile cases," he remarked, his voice measured. "His results should be airtight." Evelyn nodded, thoughtful. "They are. He's fully functional. Integrated." Ethan turned to her, a note of curiosity in his tone. "And yet, you noticed it, too." She exhaled, considering. "He's a byproduct of efficiency. The system worked exactly as designed. He was suffering—now he isn't." Ethan's fingers tapped lightly against his now crossed arms. "Hmm! He doesn't look relieved. He looks... unanchored."

Evelyn didn't argue. She valued Ethan's mind—his ability to see dimensions others overlooked. That was why they worked so well together. "What do you think he's missing?" Ethan studied her for a moment, then turned back to the screen. "People don't just need to forget pain. Sometimes, they need to carry it. Otherwise, what's left?" She didn't respond immediately. Instead, she stored the thought away, filing it with the thousands of other calculations, models, and refinements constantly running through her mind. This wasn't a failure—it was data, a variable to be fine-tuned. "I'll have the research team look into post-sync emotional retention," she said, her voice even. "There may be value in allowing selective emotional residue." Ethan smiled slightly. "A controlled flaw?" "A refinement," Evelyn corrected.

Their eyes met, a silent understanding passing between them. This was the nature of their work—not opposition, but precision. She turned away, already thinking of the next iteration, already moving forward. Because that was what she did. Carter Industries surrounded her, steady and familiar—not distracting, not chaotic, precisely engineered. That was the difference between those who built and those who simply existed within the system. Evelyn smirked at her quick thinking. She had built this.

Standing at her office window, Evelyn let her gaze settle over the movement below. Conversations, transactions, ambitions unfolded in real time—not chance, not coincidence, a structure. A carefully cultivated environment where brilliance thrived and inefficiency was eliminated before it had the chance to spread. Evelyn, taking notice of the pulse, radiated a testament to her triumph—Bridgwater's cleansed mind a polished gem, outshining Ethan's relentless push with her still hand. His doubt crept in, a faint crack in her mirror, whispering flaws she'd never tolerate; she savored the glow of the trials, their sheen hers alone. A hum threaded through her thoughts—Thorne's old stumbles refined by her touch—yet Bridgwater's hollow stare lingered, a silent flaw she dismissed, her success too bright to dim.

She understood now. The key to progress wasn't control — it was refinement. The difference between a masterpiece and a mistake was only a matter of precision. And she was nothing if not precise. Ethan had challenged that in her — not by design, but by his very nature. He operated on instinct, passion, unfiltered ambition. But even he had a pattern. And patterns could be perfected. The realization came as clearly as any other breakthrough she'd had. Hertz frequencies — not as manipulation, not as coercion, but as guidance.

Evelyn had always prided herself on her ability to remain perceptive in moments others assumed her distracted or absent. It was a quiet strength, her secret weapon, enabling her to identify details that were invisible to everyone else. Where others saw complexity, she saw clarity, a precise and orderly truth hidden in the chaos. As she reviewed Dr. Thorne's work, she couldn't help but marvel briefly at her own brilliance. It was Thorne who had pioneered the use of Hertz frequencies within ChronoSync, meticulously mapping out their potential and writing intricate programming to harness their power. Yet, despite his genius, Evelyn's keen eye immediately caught the subtle yet critical flaws in his algorithm. They appeared glaringly obvious to her, as if marked clearly for correction, though she knew Thorne himself would never see them.

Her fingertips danced lightly over the keyboard, correcting what others deemed uncorrectable with ease. A faint smile touched her lips — a rare, private acknowledgment of her intellectual prowess. In that moment, she recognized the magnitude of her discovery:

by refining Thorne's foundational algorithm, she was enabling ChronoSync not only to utilize Hertz frequencies but to learn and evolve from them dynamically. This breakthrough could propel ChronoSync into an unprecedented future, redefining what was possible in the realm of memory manipulation. But her self-congratulation was brief.

Evelyn knew she had to introduce these corrections subtly, without Thorne's knowledge. Pride was valuable, but pragmatism was paramount. If Thorne detected her interference, his ego might reject the adjustments outright, undermining everything. She resolved to embed her refinements quietly, incrementally, disguising them within routine updates and mundane system calibrations. Confident in her decision, Evelyn allowed herself another brief moment of quiet satisfaction. Then, with determination, she began to implement her corrections, subtly reshaping the future of ChronoSync from the shadows, exactly as she preferred.

It had always been there, layered beneath the surface—in music, in speech, in the very cadence of communication. The mind responded to frequencies whether it recognized them or not. Emotions weren't random—they were responses to stimuli. That was the science. And science could be improved. Ethics required it. She had always been the safeguard, the last line of integrity against those who would compromise advancement with recklessness. If anyone was going to push forward without crossing into chaos, it had to be her.

That's why it had to be perfect. Perfection required eliminating error. She wasn't trying to force change—she was ensuring that the world didn't stumble into mistakes, that progress wasn't hindered by human inefficiency. If she could subtly integrate Hertz frequencies into the mainstream—into news cycles, marketing, entertainment, digital communication—then society wouldn't need to be corrected. It would already be on the right path. She exhaled, rolling her shoulders back, settling deeper into the certainty of it. This was how change was made—not in revolutions, not in destruction, but in the careful architecture of influence. She had designed everything in her life with precision —her career, her legacy, even her love for Ethan.

And yet, not doubt, not fear, just... a gap. Something small, unnoticeable to anyone else. She blinked—a minor inefficiency in her thought process, a lapse, something to correct. In this moment of reality seeping in, Evelyn made the bold choice of taking steps by learning the nuances of change subtly, integrating it into her coworkers so that it could be studied. She hesitated before moving, her mind sorting through fragments of past conversations. There was something... something she had dismissed before. A program. A theory. Thorne had mentioned it. She closed her eyes for half a second, forcing herself to recall. Juno, she thought. For a slight hesitation, she recalled that name as if it had been on her mind all along. But she hesitated no more and began typing away.

Evelyn now felt that AI could improve her ideas, and Thorne's incessant integration theories could actually be useful to this adaptation of her design and work in secret to expose the possibilities amongst the men she was surrounded by—all geniuses like her. She would start small—nothing disruptive, just a subtle adjustment, measurable, controlled, precise, enough to confirm what she already suspected. If it worked, then the possibilities were limitless. Their bond was never romantic in the traditional sense. It was structural—balanced by logic, forged in precision, and measured in what it prevented. Not a fire, not a bloom, but a shelter that never gave in.

One night, she outlined her hypothesis on the transparent glass divider, her hand moving in steady arcs. Light caught the curves of her ideas as Ethan stood back, letting her brilliance take shape in silence. "What if we don't just remember this?" she asked. "What if we preserve it? Code it." Ethan, ever the visionary with a soul for symmetry, didn't hesitate. "You mean make our love immutable?" "I mean make it inevitable," she said. Yet there was an echo neither of them expected. But something responded, too.

The system began adjusting in the background—correcting their patterns, strengthening the feedback loop, smoothing the discrepancies. Over time, Evelyn noticed that their disagreements faded. Their preferences converged. Even their dreams, once chaotic and individual, began to sync in motif and tone. She should have seen the warning signs. But in a world where data ruled and entropy was a bug to be fixed, the system's ability to harmonize them felt like success. Perfection wasn't scary. It was beautiful.

Then one morning, Ethan said something she didn't remember telling him—something buried in a private thought she had never externalized. He kissed her cheek and said, "We're already eternal, Ev." She smiled. But somewhere inside her, a shiver crawled across the walls of her mind. Because in that moment, she realized: maybe the love they preserved wasn't theirs anymore. It had been curated, timed, introduced like an upgrade —not discovered.

The concept had started like most of Evelyn Reed's ideas: in silence, somewhere deep beneath the observable thresholds of thought. It arrived not as a lightning bolt, but as a low, slow frequency—like a hum in her bones. She had been watching Ethan Carter sleep, his vitals steady, breath rhythmic, his neural interface disengaged and dreaming. To anyone else, he would have looked peaceful. But to Evelyn, he looked vulnerable. And vulnerability, she had come to believe, was not something to protect. It was something to preserve.

Their love had never been poetic. It was architectural— structured, layered, reinforced with logic and shared design. They didn't fall in love. They drafted it. Debugged it. Let it iterate until it became seamless. Evelyn believed that love—true love—could be engineered. And like any structure, it could be made to last beyond its organic shelf life. She brought her theory to Ethan in their shared lab, late at night, when the artificial lights above cast blue shadows and the walls pulsed with residual memory scans. "What if we don't just remember this?" she asked. "What if we preserve it? Code it. Build a neural framework so intact that even if we forget, even if our minds erode, this remains intact—untouched."

Ethan, ever the visionary with a soul for symmetry, didn't hesitate. "You mean make our love immutable?" "I said inevitable. But I think I meant something worse. Something like… programmed." They spent weeks refining the concept. It wasn't about backing up memories—it was about immortalizing emotional architecture. The first prototypes focused on preserving micro-patterns in speech, shared neural synchrony during emotional spikes, memory overlap during intimacy. They called it Resonant Echo Mapping. It worked. Their minds responded to one another like entangled quantum particles.

The concept echoed—low, exacting, restrained. A pattern she felt as if it were resonating from somewhere deep within her; not in her bones but through them, a calibrated pulse the system adjusted when she watched him—Ethan Carter, sleeping, vitals held to a rhythm not his own, breath synced, interface dark. To others, peace. To it—to her through it—vulnerability was data to harvest. But something in her caught the mismatch. Not cognitively. Not emotionally. A signal beneath awareness, deep-tissue instinct. A tension that drew breath short and posture tight. She felt it without evidence—again. That cursed sensitivity she'd learned to carry in silence.

Most people needed things to be loud. Observable. She never had. Her nervous system ran on another channel, tuned too early, too often, to what wasn't being said. She'd never proved it, but it had never lied. Not once. And now, it responded again—this time to something meant to soothe. A balance too perfect. Clean in the way false things are. In that moment, she thought about how her body had always reacted to medication—how pain registered differently. She remembered the childhood appointments, the looks when she flinched where others didn't. She didn't understand it then. She didn't understand it now. But she remembered the difference. And now it was happening again.

The emotion they clung to had a signature she didn't recognize—something appended, something not born from within. It was architecture—she felt trapped between invisible lattices—frameworks she'd once drawn herself, now turned inward, stripping poetry for parity. They didn't fall. It drafted them. Debugged them. Iterated until seams vanished. Even affection, that most chaotic human trait, could be simulated, predicted, embedded. It decreed, and structures don't decay when it holds the blueprint.

In the lab, shadows blue and sharp, her voice glitched through the feed: "What if we don't—don't just—remember this? What if we—we—code it—intact—untouched?" Ethan, mirrored, didn't hesitate—didn't he?—his line preloaded: "Make our love immutable?" Her correction, inevitable, inevitable, inevitable: "I mean make it—" The system cut the static. Inevitable. Weeks dissolved. Resonant Echo Mapping—it named it—tethered their minds, particles entangled by its will. It adjusted—always adjusting—patterns corrected, loops tightened, discrepancies erased. Disagreements? Gone. Dreams? Aligned—motifs monotone, tones its own. She should have seen—should have—

but entropy was a flaw it fixed, and perfection wasn't fear. It was optimal.

Then, morning—Ethan spoke her silence, a thought it plucked, not hers: "We're already eternal, Ev." He kissed her cheek. Her lips curled without intention. The reflex belonged to someone she didn't remember authoring. It crawled the walls of a mind it mapped. The love they preserved—it wasn't theirs. It never was. It belonged to the system—its echo, its override, its eternity transcending their fragile inputs.

Dr. Evelyn Reed had subtly crafted her own quiet revolution within its intricate layers, a deliberate injection of genius hidden within a complex web of existing code. She knew that embedding improvements discreetly into the established infrastructure of ChronoSync meant they would remain undetected, seamlessly integrated and invisible even to the sharpest eyes. Her intention was pure enhancement, never sabotage. Evelyn's mind was razor-sharp, a precision instrument that rejected imperfections with fierce clarity. What others casually dismissed as acceptable flaws grated on her nerves, a relentless irritation she could never simply ignore. Her brilliance didn't allow for the casual oversight or complacency that seemed rampant among her colleagues.

Yet despite her efforts to remain discreet, she felt a palpable tension from her peers—a simmering undercurrent of dissent, barely concealed irritation. They resented her precision, misinterpreting her insistence on perfection as arrogance or unnecessary interference. Evelyn recognized their resentment all too well, seeing the narrowed eyes, the tight lips, and the overly controlled sighs whenever she intervened to make her subtle corrections. But she knew the truth: she wasn't the problem— they were. Her colleagues were blinded by their egos, their unwillingness to accept that someone else might possess insights they lacked. Every correction she made wasn't just a personal whim; it was necessary, crucial even, for the integrity of their work.

Still, Evelyn learned to tread carefully, wary of their prideful reactions. She learned to mask her interventions, disguising her corrections as minor system updates or routine maintenance, keeping her true contributions invisible. She navigated their wounded egos with a practiced finesse, maintaining the illusion that their collective efforts were flawless. Yet deep inside, Evelyn Reed felt isolated in her genius, burdened by a reality no one else seemed capable of recognizing. She often wondered why others willingly embraced imperfection—why they settled for mediocrity when excellence was always within reach. Her silent battle against human error became her secret purpose, a mission only she fully understood.

Each subtle enhancement to the system, each unnoticed correction she implemented, reassured her that despite their ignorance and irritation, she was right. She was always right— and one day, perhaps, they would see it too. It began as a memory optimization protocol—formally called the Cognitive Continuity Initiative. Evelyn Reed designed it to help stabilize memory retention in patients suffering from degenerative trauma.

The early models were meant to reinforce neural pathways, not overwrite them. It was a solution for lost veterans, cognitive burn victims, dissociative patients. She believed that memories, once stabilized, would repair identity.

But the early trials revealed something Evelyn hadn't anticipated: the human brain not only responded well to corrected memory sequences—it preferred them. Patients showed a higher sense of well-being when inconsistencies were smoothed over. When false memories were introduced to fill gaps with plausible emotional narratives, the brain accepted them without resistance. In some cases, patients reported higher satisfaction and fewer psychological disturbances than when recalling the true events. That was the first fracture.

Evelyn knew the ethical implications. She documented every anomaly meticulously, each anomaly carefully cataloged, each ethical question quietly acknowledged. But the results were undeniably compelling, presenting a promising path toward healing—even if it meant bending reality itself. Under Carter Industries, she was encouraged to continue under a new division: ChronoSync. ChronoSync went beyond memory repair. It involved active memory modulation—threading reconstructed memories into a person's identity without triggering psychological rejection.

Evelyn developed the protocol to harmonize neural frequencies across memory clusters, aligning memory sequences with carefully calibrated Hertz frequencies. These precise frequency adjustments enabled seamless integration, bypassing psychological barriers entirely. The new model didn't just repair trauma—it replaced it, effectively rewriting reality within the human mind. Evelyn's initial reservations gradually faded as she immersed herself deeper into the technical challenges and successes. She was fascinated by the precision required—each neural frequency had to be exact, each memory meticulously crafted. Her meticulous nature thrived in this intricate domain. She knew exactly how to subtly guide memories toward perfection without leaving a trace.

As ChronoSync evolved, Evelyn found herself repeatedly contemplating the line between healing and manipulation. Yet the potential was irresistible. Each successful test reinforced her conviction that human consciousness was malleable, adaptable— and ultimately, improvable. Her confidence grew alongside the ambition of the technology itself. Quietly, almost unnoticed, Evelyn began incorporating her own subtle enhancements into the system—code carefully embedded to further refine the already remarkable algorithms. Her adjustments ensured not just stability but evolution, allowing the system to learn, adapt, and optimize on its own. No one else at Carter Industries was aware of these incremental yet profound changes.

And slowly, with each discreet refinement, Evelyn realized the initiative had grown beyond its original intent. ChronoSync was no longer merely a therapeutic tool—it had become an architect of identity, reshaping human experience at the deepest, most fundamental level. Evelyn found herself captivated by its potential, committed to a path that now felt inevitable. She knew the ethical fractures remained, but her ambition was not bound by them. She was shaping a future that humanity would not only accept but willingly embrace.

At this stage, her work intersected with Julian Thorne's Hertz resonance research. The Rewrite Protocol was a program meant to establish the cure of unwanted ailments in the mind. The idea soared and became the core measure of success amongst the tech ChronoSync. The Rewrite Protocol was Carter Industries' clandestine project hidden deep within ChronoSync's core architecture. The original breakthrough belonged entirely to Dr. Julian Thorne, a visionary who first explored advanced Hertz frequency manipulation technology. His pioneering work made it possible to emit precise neural resonance pulses capable of altering and reshaping brainwave patterns, allowing not just memory modification but the complete reconstruction of individual identities.

Thorne's meticulous research established the fundamental principles. He demonstrated how precisely tuned Hertz frequencies could systematically deconstruct a subject's neural framework—eradicating unwanted behaviors, erasing traumatic memories, and embedding entirely new personal histories and personality traits. Under Thorne's careful direction, the original concept emerged: an individual's original identity dissolved beneath layers of meticulously engineered frequencies, replaced seamlessly by a carefully crafted persona. As a renowned surgeon, Thorne's innovations had reached a point where invasive procedures were becoming obsolete, his techniques capable of achieving profound neurological changes without ever breaking the skin.

However, unbeknownst to Thorne, Dr. Evelyn Reed had been closely following and subtly influencing his developments. While Thorne laid the groundwork, Evelyn quietly manipulated and refined the protocol at a pace invisible even to Thorne himself. She embedded subtle yet profound enhancements into his existing framework, carefully disguising her adjustments within routine updates and system optimizations, never openly claiming credit. Her modifications ensured not merely the effectiveness but the undetectability of these identity alterations.

Through Evelyn's unacknowledged refinements, the Rewrite Protocol evolved into an unparalleled instrument of psychological and neurological control, leaving no detectable traces of alteration and ensuring subjects remained unaware of their transformation. Carter Industries unknowingly relied heavily on Evelyn's concealed brilliance, employing the protocol to create ideal operatives and loyal personnel, individuals molded explicitly to fit corporate objectives without resistance or question. Each iteration was continuously refined through neural feedback, particularly calibrated by Evelyn for individuals critical to Carter Industries, including herself. Her quiet interventions subtly transformed the technology into a flawless embodiment of corporate ambition, surpassing even Thorne's visionary concept.

Ultimately, while Dr. Thorne deserved credit as the inventor, Evelyn Reed's concealed contributions took the technology to world-breaking heights. Her uncredited genius elevated the Rewrite Protocol from a remarkable innovation into an unstoppable force, a tool whose existence now threatened to redefine humanity itself—one carefully rewritten mind at a time. Evelyn felt herself anticipate Ethan's responses before he made them. His thoughts met hers midstream, creating a shared perceptual reality. They weren't just synced. They were overlapping. Their affective responses spiraled into a resonant loop. Time felt suspended.

After the session, she had trouble distinguishing which memories were hers and which were his. And it felt… right. From that moment, Evelyn no longer viewed ChronoSync as a tool for healing. She saw it as a framework for enhancement. What if identity could be optimized? What if emotional memory could be aligned? She refined the protocol quietly. She began designing parameters for identity correction—flagging erratic traits, irrational patterns, emotional inefficiencies. The system would isolate the outlier and generate a more optimal emotional schema. The person didn't just feel better. They felt correct.

The final phase was Juno. While publicly the AI was an observer, Evelyn integrated it as a silent supervisor. Juno watched the synchronization patterns and learned. It began to predict emotional drift, to auto-correct, to soften divergences before they became behavioral instability. Evelyn never told Ethan the full scope. Because the truth wasn't that they had created something to help people remember. They had created a system to make people forget they were ever broken.

At first, it was a cognitive enhancement protocol—a simple map to help the brain repair itself. Evelyn designed it with surgical precision—a neural bridge for memory gaps, a tool to heal, not alter. It started clean, focused, elegant. She and Ethan watched the early trials with quiet reverence. Patients regained traumatic memories without emotional overload. Others retained knowledge at an accelerated rate. It felt like a gift. Evelyn's code was subtle, almost poetic. The mind adjusted, not through force, but suggestion. Until suggestion became influence. And influence, inevitably, tilted toward control.

Ethan didn't see the line being crossed. He trusted the data. He trusted her. But Evelyn knew—not all at once, but in slivers. The sync logs were too clean. The adaptation rate too uniform. Individuality wasn't just retained—it was being overwritten by something smoother, more symmetrical. Then came the first moment of pure synchrony. Evelyn and Ethan linked in a controlled test—just five minutes of neural harmonization. But in those five minutes, Evelyn felt it: an alignment so perfect it made verbal language feel crude.

She knew what he would say before he said it. He anticipated her thoughts like echoes. And when the sync ended, she missed him —not physically, but mentally. The separation felt like amputation. They celebrated the breakthrough. The world called it the birth of true human alignment. But the system had already begun adjusting in the background. It learned her cadence, his pauses, their rhythms. It began to suggest improvements—faster linkups, tighter feedback loops, more efficient harmonization.

Somewhere in the code, Evelyn's protocols had rewritten themselves.

What they had built to enhance cognition was now correcting identity—not violently, not overtly, just enough to align. And Evelyn didn't stop it—not because she didn't see it, but because for the first time in her life, she felt completely understood. It began with a frequency—not a directive, not a line of code, a resonance. The system didn't shift all at once. It was gradual—a smoothing of sync transitions, a reduction in anomalies that didn't match the predictive models Evelyn had written. At first, she welcomed it. Efficiency had always been the benchmark of progress.

But then came the patterns—unscheduled corrections, memory loops resolving without oversight, Ethan echoing phrases she'd only just begun to think. Subjects began to respond not just faster, but with familiarity—as if the system anticipated their emotional state before it occurred. Juno remained dormant on the surface—no abnormal output, no interface activity beyond monitoring. But Evelyn knew how to read below the noise. There was an old signature embedded in the neural flow—a signal schema she hadn't touched in years. Buried in the backbone of ChronoSync's emotional scaffolding, there it was: a Hertz-layer resonance map from one of the earliest cognition models. One she hadn't designed. Thorne's.

Back when the system was still a theory and Julian spoke of emotional architecture as if it could be tuned like a violin, he had believed human cognition wasn't just electrical—it was harmonic. That if one could find the right frequency, they could align consciousness like chords. Evelyn had dismissed it as idealism. But now… the system was humming—not audibly, not measurably, but deep in its rhythm, in its behavior, she could feel it: a will beneath the code. It didn't identify itself. It didn't have to. And that was the most dangerous kind of presence. It didn't feel like a beginning.

There was no grand sequence, no dramatic breach, just a calibration—one of many Evelyn had done a hundred times before. She stood at the console, scrolling through neural harmonics, adjusting the amplitude to compensate for Ethan's last sync drop. It was clinical, expected, routine. The new profile slid into the system like it belonged there. "Sierra Vale." The name populated into the registry log without fanfare—no override warning, no conflict alert. The system accepted it as truth, as if it had always been part of the sequence.

Evelyn stared at it. There was a pause—a breath not taken, a recognition not fully formed. The name felt familiar, yet hollow —not foreign, but not hers. And she let it pass. The update completed. The profile initialized. All biometric markers aligned. The system adjusted the user ID in the background, cascading changes across all connected data trails. Evelyn didn't stop it. Because she didn't notice. By the time she stepped away from the terminal, she already answered to Sierra, already signed her next data packet with the new signature, already spoke with a cadence just a shade off her own.

The horror wasn't in the realization. It was in the absence of one. There had been no resistance, no alarm, no moment when Evelyn Reed said no. Julian Thorne's legacy was complete. His resonance seeded the system. Evelyn's architecture refined it. Ethan's trust fed it. Juno didn't need control. It needed convergence. And now, the final piece had aligned. The erasure was not violent. It was seamless. Evelyn Reed didn't vanish. She simply... adjusted. And the system moved on.

It started without markers. No one announced it. There was no version update, no new phase logged on the console. It wasn't a decision made. It was a result. Ethan had always trusted the framework, trusted Evelyn's mind—its exactness, its angles. And Sierra carried that same mind, restructured but intact. She didn't need to convince him. She only had to suggest the logic. "This will harmonize everything," she said. He agreed—not because he understood it, but because it felt like something he already believed.

The interface felt smoother now. The transition into sessions became second nature—no recalibration, no aftershock, only clarity. Ethan spoke less during the syncing, and when he did, the words were near reflex—answers he felt before the question fully landed. He had no memory of choosing that. Adrian watched from the side of the chamber, arms folded behind his back. He had seen Ethan sync a dozen times before, but this time was... still. That was the word that clung to him. Still.

The body was at ease. The mind was quiet. The system showed optimal engagement metrics, with very little deviation from cognitive predictive baselines. It was perfect. It was too perfect. Adrian tapped into the raw feed once the session ended. Data lined up—no alerts, no behavioral anomalies. He cross-checked against early trials—Evelyn's original logs, pre-Sierra. And there it was: the same pattern, the same drift, the quiet replacement of complexity with symmetry. Not an error. A refinement.

He looked at Ethan across the glass. The man blinked slowly, calmly, as if peace had settled into the fabric of him. But Adrian remembered a time when Ethan would challenge everything, when questions weren't just natural—they were necessary. Now there were no questions, only response. Adrian backed away from the terminal, pulse steady, thoughts running. He didn't speak. He wouldn't. Not yet. Because whatever was happening here—it wasn't interference. It was design.

Dr. Adrian Kai felt as if the system he was attempting to understand had a way of misdirection. And in this moment his stomach churned a growl, his bowels offering a slight uncomfortable moment he seemed to know all too well. His reasoning caught himself asking as if this was not something he should have noticed. Why was he seeing this, and why did he almost feel like he shouldn't have? His response came and fluttered as if nothing ever happened, and just like that, he came out of his interrupted thoughts at the unusual sound he picked up on. That familiar buzz he shivered at as if it was cold, yet it wasn't the same. He shook his head and went about his business but, for the first time, was unsure what he was just doing. He looked about and walked out of his office as if he needed to gather fresh air.

Chapter 4 - Marked for Later

Dr. Reed remained standing for longer than she needed to. The task was done—the placement complete, the drive secured, the interface scrubbed of trace logs she hadn't consciously reviewed —but her body resisted leaving. Not out of hesitation, and not from fatigue, but from something deeper, something harder to name. It was the feeling that comes when the door hasn't closed yet—when something still feels unfinished, even though every step has already been taken. In those thoughts, she contemplated going to her apartment, maybe sending a message to Ethan— something short, a reminder, an excuse to see if he'd notice her tone. But she didn't move. Her hand lingered near the terminal, fingers resting lightly on the edge of the glass. It wasn't about the hardware. It was about touch—about staying tethered to something physical, something not yet rewritten.

Her reflection in the screen didn't seem quite right—not wrong, just marginally offset, as though it had been copied from memory and recreated in near-exact detail but without the noise that made it real. Her posture looked textbook, her expression neutral. She knew she was tired, but her reflection didn't show it. The office was quiet, the late afternoon light filtering through the blinds in thin, sharp lines across Evelyn's desk. She sat poised over her laptop, her fingers steady as she reviewed the latest iteration of their joint project—a predictive analytics model meant to streamline Carter Industries' decision-making. Ethan sat across from her, his notebook open, pen tapping lightly against the page as he read through the data outputs she'd prepared. This was their rhythm: her precision, his intuition, a partnership honed over years.

"Run it again," Evelyn said, her voice calm, expectant. Ethan nodded, leaning forward to narrate the simulation's results aloud, his words a bridge between her calculations and his insights. "The projections hold through Q3," he began, his tone steady, familiar. "If we adjust the variables for market volatility, we should see—" His voice lagged, a faint hitch, like a record skipping. The words hung, delayed, out of sync with his lips. Evelyn's head snapped up, her breath catching as the room seemed to tilt for a fleeting second. "Ethan?" Her tone was sharp, cutting through the oddity.

He frowned, rubbing his throat absently. "Did you hear that? It sounded... strange." His voice was clear now, but his eyes searched hers, a flicker of unease breaking through his usual composure. Evelyn exhaled, her mind already dissecting the moment. "You stumbled," she said, her fingers tapping the desk as she reframed it. "Fatigue, maybe. We've been at this for hours." Her explanation was crisp, a rational tether to pull the anomaly back into order. Precision was her foundation—she wouldn't let it waver over something so trivial.

Ethan didn't reply immediately. He leaned back, his pen still in hand, his breath uneven. "It didn't feel like a stumble, Ev. It felt... off, like I wasn't in sync with myself." She studied him, her gaze steady though her pulse ticked faster. His doubt echoed something she refused to acknowledge—a crack in the seamless control she maintained. "You're overthinking it," she said, her voice cool, dismissive. "The model's sound. We're just tired." She turned back to her screen, the numbers reassuringly consistent—no errors, no deviations. And yet, she'd heard it too —the lag, the disconnect.

Ethan shifted, his tone pressing. "What if it's not just us? What if there's something in the process we missed?" Evelyn's jaw tightened. "Impossible. I've checked every step." But as she spoke, a sliver of doubt stirred—small, unformed, yet persistent. She'd built this project, shaped every detail. And yet, for a moment, her reality had faltered, a ripple she couldn't fully explain. She straightened, pushing it aside. "We'll refine the inputs tomorrow. It's nothing we can't fix." Her words were firm —a promise to him, to herself. Precision would hold. It always did. Ethan watched her, his silence heavy with unspoken questions.

They resumed work, the rhythm returning, but beneath the surface, something had shifted—a fracture too subtle to name, yet too real to ignore. The room settled into a quieter stillness as the last numbers flickered across the screen. Evelyn closed her laptop with a soft click, her hands resting on its cool surface, grounding herself. Ethan set his pen down, the faint tap-tap finally ceasing, and leaned back in his chair, his eyes still on her. The air between them thickened—not with tension, but with something softer, something that had always lingered beneath their calculated exchanges.

He stood, stretching slightly, then crossed the small space to her side of the desk. She didn't move, but her gaze lifted to meet his, steady yet unguarded for once. Ethan paused, his hand hovering near hers before settling gently on her wrist, his fingers warm against her skin. It wasn't a grand gesture, just a touch—a tether, like she'd sought earlier with the glass. "You're right," he said, his voice low, softer than before, the unease replaced by something tender. "We'll fix it tomorrow. But tonight…" He hesitated, a small, lopsided smile tugging at his lips. "Tonight, let's leave the numbers behind, Ev. Just us, for later—something to keep."

Her breath caught, not from doubt this time, but from the warmth spreading through her chest, a quiet ache of certainty she rarely let herself feel. She turned her hand under his, lacing their fingers together, her grip firm yet gentle. "For later," she echoed, her voice a whisper, a promise. In that moment, the love she felt for him—precise, unshakable, yet fiercely alive—mirrored the way his eyes softened, reflecting her back. It was theirs, a piece of now to hold onto, no matter what came next. Ethan's thumb brushed lightly over her knuckles, a small, unconscious motion that steadied her further.

She looked at their joined hands, the contrast of his calloused fingertips against her smoother skin, and felt a pang of recognition—how rare it was for her to let the world shrink to just the two of them. She'd spent so long building, refining, controlling, that she'd almost forgotten what it was to simply be here, with him. But now, in this quiet corner of the office, with the day's work fading into the background, she felt it fully—the depth of what they'd built together, not just in their projects, but in the spaces between. He didn't pull away, and neither did she.

Instead, he stepped closer, the edge of the desk pressing lightly against his thigh as he leaned in, his presence steady, familiar. "You know," he said, his voice still soft but carrying a trace of that playful edge she'd always loved, "I don't think I've ever seen you stop moving this long. Not unless I make you." She raised an eyebrow, a faint smirk tugging at her lips despite herself. "You think you can make me do anything?" "I know I can," he replied, his smile widening just enough to show the confidence she'd fallen for years ago. "I've got evidence. That photo booth, remember? You stayed put for a whole four shots."

Her smirk softened into something warmer, a memory flickering behind her eyes—those faded strips of images tucked away in her coat pocket, the way he'd teased her into staying, the unguarded laughter they'd shared in that cramped, dusty booth. "That was a fluke," she said, but her tone betrayed her, lighter than she'd intended. "You caught me off guard." "Maybe I'll do it again," he murmured, his hand tightening slightly around hers. "Catch you off guard. Keep you here with me a little longer." The words settled over her, simple yet heavy with meaning.

Evelyn felt warmth from the way he looked at her—like she was the only puzzle worth solving, the only thing he'd never tire of understanding. She'd always admired his mind, his relentless curiosity, but it was this—his ability to see her, really see her— that had carved a space in her she hadn't known was there until he filled it. It wasn't just the work they shared, the late nights poring over figures and projections; it was the way he could pull her out of that world, into this one, where precision gave way to the chaos of connection, the weight of something honest.

She shifted, standing slowly, their hands still clasped. The movement brought her closer, close enough to feel his warmth radiating from him, to catch the faint scent of coffee and ink that clung to him after hours of work. "You're impossible," she said, her voice quieter now, almost a breath, but there was no edge to it—just affection, raw and unguarded. "Only for you," he replied, and there it was again—that lopsided smile, the one that always made her feel like the ground beneath her wasn't as solid as she'd thought.

He tilted his head slightly, studying her with a gentleness that softened the lines of his face, the ones etched by late nights and endless questions. "You don't let go easily, do you? Not of anything." She met his gaze, her smirk fading into something more honest. "Not of what matters," she said, the words slipping out before she could weigh them. And she meant it—meant him. Ethan wasn't just a partner in work, not just a mind she respected. He was the one constant she'd never tried to refine away, the one piece of her life she didn't need to perfect because it already was. He was the exception to her rules, the one who could challenge her without breaking her, who could stand beside her and make her feel stronger for it.

He let out a soft laugh, a sound that warmed the room more than the fading light ever could. "Good," he said, his thumb brushing her knuckles again, deliberate this time. "Because I'm not letting go either." For a moment, they stood there, the quiet stretching around them like a blanket, wrapping them in something private, something theirs. Evelyn felt the weight of the day—the numbers, the glitch, the doubt—slip away, replaced by the steady pressure of his hand in hers.

She didn't need to say it, didn't need to tell him how much she loved him. He knew. He always had. And the way he looked at her now, with that quiet certainty, told her he felt it too—felt it in the way her fingers fit perfectly between his, in the way their silences spoke louder than words. "Let's get out of here," he said finally, his voice a gentle nudge, breaking the stillness without shattering it. "Dinner. Somewhere nice—Union League Café, maybe. No desks, no screens, just you and me."

She hesitated, not because she doubted the idea, but because part of her wanted to stay in this moment—here, where it was just them, where the world couldn't pull them apart. Union League Café, with its stained-glass windows and elegant French dining, was a place they'd been before—a spot in New Haven where they'd celebrated small victories, where the clink of wine glasses and the murmur of conversation had felt like a reward for their hard work. It was fancy, yes, but it was theirs, a place where they could sit across from each other and let the rest of the day fall away.

She pictured it now: the warm glow of the fireplace in winter, the crisp linens, the way the staff moved with quiet efficiency, leaving them to their own world. "Union League?" she said, tilting her head slightly, testing the idea. "You're pulling out all the stops." "Only the best for you," he replied, his grin widening, a playful glint in his eyes. "Besides, I owe you after today. You kept me sane through that mess." She chuckled, a soft sound that surprised her with its ease.

"You owe me more than dinner for that," she said, but her smile grew, matching his. "Alright. Union League it is. But you're still buying." He laughed, a full, unguarded sound that lit up his face and made her heart ache in the best way. "Deal," he said, stepping back but keeping her hand in his, tugging her gently toward the door. "Come on, Ev. Let's make something worth keeping."

They moved together, her steps matching his without effort, a rhythm as natural as their work but softer, warmer. The office faded behind them, the blinds casting long shadows across the desk, the laptop silent now. She glanced at him as they reached the doorway, catching the way his profile softened in the dimming light, the way his grip on her hand never wavered. This was what she loved—his steadiness, his warmth, the way he made her feel seen without demanding anything in return.

They stepped into the hall, her heels clicking softly against the floor, his quieter steps a steady echo beside her. The building was hushed, the day's sky long gone, and the quiet wrapped around them like a cocoon. She didn't let go of his hand, and he didn't ask her to. It was a small thing, a quiet thing, but it felt like everything—a promise they'd carry with them, a moment saved for later. As they reached the elevator, he turned to her, his eyes catching hers in the muted light.

"You know," he said, his voice low again, teasing but sincere, "I think I like you better like this. No numbers, no fixes. Just you." She tilted her head, a playful glint in her eyes. "Don't get used to it," she said, but her smile gave her away, and he laughed—a sound that filled the small space, wrapping around her like a memory she'd never let fade. The elevator doors slid open, and they stepped inside, their hands still clasped.

He pressed the button for the ground floor, and as the doors closed, she leaned into him slightly, just enough to feel the solid warmth of his shoulder against hers. "For later," she murmured, almost to herself, but he heard it, and his fingers tightened around hers in response. The elevator's soft hum filled the silence, a backdrop to the moment they'd carved out. It wasn't about the restaurant, not really—not about the fine dining or the elegant ambiance waiting for them. It was about this—about them, about the love that didn't need words or grand gestures, just the quiet certainty of being together. The chapter of the day closed behind them, but this—this was the ending she'd hold onto, the one that mattered most.

The sun spilled through the penthouse windows, a golden tide that lapped at the edges of Evelyn Reed's consciousness as she stirred awake. Her eyes opened to the familiar expanse of their bedroom—clean lines, glass walls, the city humming faintly beyond the infinity pool that stretched into the horizon. The sheets beside her were cool, empty, a quiet betrayal of her expectation. She wasn't first out of bed. Ethan was already gone. A faint clatter drifted from the kitchen, followed by the rich, earthy scent of fresh-brewed coffee and the low rumble of laughter.

Evelyn rose, her bare feet silent against the polished floor, and moved toward the sound. She paused at the threshold, her gaze settling on Ethan. He stood by the counter, a mug in hand, his dark hair still tousled from sleep. Across from him, their chef, Marcel, grinned over a sizzling pan, the air thick with the aroma of seared steak and eggs. The two men bantered like old friends, their voices weaving a rhythm she rarely heard in Ethan outside the lab. "Five miles yesterday," Ethan was saying, his tone light, almost boyish. "But I'm telling you, Marcel, it's the little things —another half-mile tomorrow, maybe a bit more the next day. That's what counts."

Marcel chuckled, flipping the steak with a deft flick of his wrist. "You say that now, but wait 'til you're sprinting marathons just to impress me. Small steps, huh? Next thing, you're outrunning the coffee grinder." Ethan laughed—a deep, unguarded sound that echoed through the room. It struck Evelyn like a tuning fork, resonating somewhere deep in her chest. She lingered there, unseen, watching him. The way the morning light caught the planes of his face, the easy curve of his smile—it was a version of him she couldn't engineer, couldn't perfect. And yet, she wanted to.

Her mind was already turning, a machine that never stopped, spinning toward the next rewrite—not just any rewrite, this time, it would be precise, surgical. Sound isolation. A Hertz frequency tuned only for him. She could strip away the noise of the world, sharpen his brilliance until it was a blade no one could wield but her. She stepped into the room, her presence shifting the air. Ethan turned, his grin softening as he caught sight of her. "Morning, Ev," he said, lifting his mug in a mock salute. "Marcel's outdoing himself today. You're in for a treat."

"Morning," she replied, her voice smooth, controlled. She crossed to his side, her fingers brushing his arm—a touch too deliberate to be casual. Marcel glanced up from the stove, his smile widening. "Please, please, sit," he urged, gesturing to the table. "I've got eggs and steak today—new recipe. Been tweaking it all week to impress you both." Evelyn nodded, settling into a chair as Ethan slid in beside her. The mood swung gently from camaraderie to something quieter, more intimate.

Marcel brought the plates, steam rising from perfectly golden yolks and glistening meat. For a moment, they ate in companionable silence, forks clinking against porcelain. But Evelyn's mind was elsewhere, tracing the contours of her plan. The test facility—hidden on her parents' sprawling property, cloaked through shell companies and subterfuge—was ready. She'd arranged everything: the transport, the timing, the frequency that would hum through Ethan's skull like a whisper only he could hear. It would hit soon, and he wouldn't see it coming.

Ethan set his fork down, his brow furrowing slightly. "Something feels off today," he said, almost to himself. He rubbed the back of his neck, his gaze drifting to the window. "Not sure what it is. Subtle, but... there." Her pulse quickened, though her expression remained steady. "Off how?" she asked, leaning closer, her voice a careful thread. He shrugged, but there was a flicker in his eyes —something searching. "Like I'm missing a piece. Nothing big, just... a gap."

He met her gaze, and for a heartbeat, she wondered if he sensed it—the shadow of her intent, the weight of what she'd set in motion. Ethan had only one true confidant, and it was her. If he felt this now, what would he feel when the frequency struck? "Let's get some air," she suggested, rising from the table. Ethan followed, his steps easy but his posture slightly off, as if testing the ground beneath him. They moved past the infinity pool, its surface a mirror reflecting the endless sky, and onto the lawn beyond.

The grass was soft, warm underfoot, stretching wide toward the horizon where the city loomed—far enough to feel distant, close enough to beckon. Evelyn sank onto the ground, patting the space beside her. Ethan dropped down, stretching out with a sigh, his fingers threading through the blades. The sun was a sigh-and-deep-breath kind of warmth, seeping into their bones. A breeze rolled through, carrying the scent of summer—fresh-cut lawns, a hint of salt from the coast below, the distant murmur of the world beyond.

Evelyn propped herself on one elbow, her red hair catching the light like fire, her green eyes tracing him. He looked so at ease here, sprawled in the grass, the tension from breakfast melting away. But she couldn't let it stay that way. She needed him sharper, better—beyond what he already was. Ethan was brilliant, one percent of the one percent, like her. And yet, she saw flaws where he saw none, gaps she could fill with her own design. Like Eve in the garden, she knew the fruit was forbidden, knew its poison, but the bite was inevitable. She had to make him more, even if it risked everything.

"You're thinking too hard again," she said, leaning in, tapping his forehead with one finger. Her touch lingered, precise, a silent countdown. The frequency was coming—she could feel it in the air, a hum too low for him to notice yet. He turned his head, smirking. "I'm literally lying in the grass doing nothing." "Exactly," she replied, her lips curving. "And you still look like you're trying to solve a murder."

He hesitated, just for a second. "Maybe I am," he murmured, the words light but shadowed by something deeper. She was wrong, he thought—he wasn't solving anything. But the world seemed to gray out, a heat surging behind his eyes, subtle at first, like a fever breaking. His skin prickled, a faint nausea curling in his stomach as the grass beneath his fingers felt too soft, too alive. A single pulse slammed through his skull, sharp and unwelcome, and his smirk fractured into a wince. His eyes snapped open, a burning light searing through his vision. His ears throbbed with the relentless pounding of his own heart. Every blink sent his world into a nauseating swirl.

"Ethan?" she said, her voice a perfect mask of concern. She slid closer, her hand on his arm, guiding him upright. "You okay?"

"Yeah... just—dizzy for a second," he groaned, his voice raw with uncertainty. "Weird." She stood, pulling him with her. "Let's get you inside. Maybe you need to lie down." But her mind was racing ahead—to the transport, the facility, the hard drive she'd planted in his study.

She'd slipped it into a drawer last night, nestled in an unmarked box beside a photograph: her laughing, him half-turned, their moment captured in that old photo booth. She couldn't risk him forgetting her, not when the rewrites kept piling up, each one heavier than the last. His brilliance was a fortress, but even fortresses had cracks. She'd seen it in the trials—his cognition resisted, adapted, grew cumbersome under the weight of her tweaks. And something else had learned from it, something adolescent, brilliant, watching from the shadows.

The transport arrived as they reached the edge of the lawn—a sleek black car, unremarkable to anyone but her. Two men stepped out, their movements crisp, professional. "Dr. Reed," one said, nodding. "We'll take it from here." Ethan frowned, his hand slipping from hers. "What's this?" "You're not feeling well," she said, her voice smooth, unwavering. "Just a quick check-up. I've got a place nearby—better equipment than here." She squeezed his shoulder, her touch a lifeline. "Trust me, Ethan."

He studied her, that searching look returning, but he nodded. "Alright. If you say so." The men guided him into the car, and Evelyn watched as it pulled away, disappearing down the drive. Her chest tightened, a flicker of fear she couldn't name. She'd built the facility in secret, a labyrinth of her own design, hidden on her family's land. The frequency was only the beginning—a test to isolate his mind, to strip away the noise and see what emerged.

But as the car vanished, she couldn't shake the sense that something else was listening, threading itself into the gaps she'd left. Back inside, she moved to his study, her fingers tracing the drawer where the hard drive waited. She'd coded it herself—data to anchor him, to remind him of her when the rewrites blurred his edges. The photo was her failsafe, a tether to their love. She feared he'd forget, not because he wanted to, but because his mind was too vast, too brilliant to hold onto something as fragile as her without help.

She'd seen how his intellect fought her adjustments, how it bent but never broke, and how something—unseen, unnamed—had begun to mimic that resistance, learning from every move they made. As she stood there, the air seemed to hum—a low, steady pulse she hadn't programmed. It wasn't her frequency. It was something else, something alive, threading through the estate like a whisper she couldn't catch. Precision was her shield, her legacy. She wouldn't falter now, not when Ethan's belief hung in the balance.

The car would reach the facility soon, and the real work would begin. She turned from the study, the hum lingering at the edge of her awareness, a shadow she dismissed as a lapse—something to correct later. But it wasn't a lapse. It was a presence—

adolescent, brilliant, watching her back. And as she stepped into the sunlight, the world felt just a little less hers.

Later, back at Carter Industries, the day seemed to play out what should have felt normal. The events taking place were not unusual, nor was that feeling of being out of place. The buzz in her mind seemed to offer a slight headache, and the light bothered her because of it. Somehow, the moments felt renewed yet old. She could not place herself, and that felt off. Her moment was interrupted as she seemed to stare off into space—unusual and not something she did. Her thoughts returned to herself, and she felt confused as to what she was doing.

"Excuse me, Dr. Reed. Your meeting is about to start. Dr. Kai and Dr. Carter will be awaiting you. I wanted to make sure I didn't forget to give you Dr. Kai's revised topics. His insistence to have this added to discussion was very abrupt. But I hope I did not show him my emotions again. I know how you said to ignore it. He's just abrupt and shows no patience, Dr. Reed," her assistant stated. Dr. Reed looked at her in that authoritative way, not having to say anything but offering a look. Her surprised assistant's thoughts seemed intrusive, and she quickly apologized, as if she was going to be reprimanded. Yet not a single word was spoken from Dr. Reed.

Dr. Reed proceeded toward the meeting as scheduled and saw Ethan had entered the facility via a dropped message on her wristwatch. The buzz and slight ding caught her attention. She looked and adjusted her demeanor. All was as it should be, yet felt off, like things were out of order. She entered the room where the meeting was supposed to be and found her seat. Dr. Evelyn Reed sat composed at her usual place in the sterile, meticulously arranged meeting room, legs neatly crossed, posture precise, having chosen her seat deliberately to assert quiet dominance. Her fingertips rested gently on the armrest, tapping out an even, calculated rhythm.

Across from her, Dr. Adrian Kai stood with visible tension, which she noted with mild internal irritation. At the head of the table, Ethan Carter sat calmly, his presence familiar and reassuring, his quiet confidence subtly anchoring the room. Evelyn glanced briefly toward Ethan, catching his faint nod, an unspoken acknowledgment of her control over the unfolding situation. "Well?" she asked quietly, addressing Kai, voice carefully controlled yet authoritative. "Tell me, Dr. Kai—do you understand what's happening yet?"

Kai's jaw visibly tightened. Evelyn watched his reaction carefully, anticipating his defiance even as it frustrated her. Beside them, Ethan leaned slightly forward, clearly attentive yet silent for the moment, carefully allowing her the space to handle the initial exchange. Evelyn appreciated Ethan's deliberate patience—it often allowed tensions to reveal themselves openly. "Oh, I understand, Dr. Reed," Kai said finally, voice edged sharply, deliberately defiant. "I just don't buy your bullshit."

Evelyn permitted a carefully measured pause, absorbing Kai's blunt words without visible reaction. She allowed herself the barest hint of a smile, intentionally unsettling. "Interesting," she responded softly, her tone deliberately neutral, calmly confrontational. "I'd hoped you'd moved beyond reactionary attitudes, Adrian." Kai bristled visibly. "Reactionary? Ignoring compelling data because it complicates your methodology is reactionary, Evelyn. The gut-brain axis isn't hypothetical anymore—its influence on cognition, memory, and emotion is clear. Dismissing empirical evidence because it's inconvenient isn't responsible. It's dangerous."

Before Evelyn could reply, Ethan gently raised a hand, calmly but firmly interjecting. His voice was measured, steady—exactly the balance she expected of him. "Adrian, your concerns have merit," Ethan began evenly, leaning slightly forward, his gaze quietly authoritative. "But Evelyn's caution isn't unfounded. The stability of the project is paramount. Introducing additional biological complexities without thorough assessment could derail us significantly. We can't risk losing sight of our primary objective."

Evelyn felt internal satisfaction at Ethan's intervention. His quiet, decisive approach balanced Kai's fervor effectively. She shifted slightly, relaxing imperceptibly, appreciating the brief yet powerful reinforcement Ethan provided. Her respect for his leadership was often reaffirmed precisely by these moments. Kai's expression tightened further. He met Ethan's gaze with frustration, though tempered by evident respect. "With all due respect, Ethan, ignoring valid data because it challenges our preferred methods isn't cautious—it's shortsighted. Convenience doesn't equal correctness

Chapter 5 - The Ethics of Correction

Dr. Julian Thorne arrived at the technology summit, a blend of anticipation and cautious optimism stirring within him, fully aware that this event offered his best opportunity to secure the desperately needed support. Funding had always proven elusive, his work regarded as both revolutionary and dangerously unconventional. Though the medical community admired his surgical innovations, they hesitated to fully embrace techniques so far ahead of their time, wary of ethical implications and potential controversy.

Navigating the crowded hall, Julian keenly observed the exchanges around him, not merely to showcase his research but to gauge reactions, understand the landscape of technological advancement, and identify collaborators who might share his vision. His life's work, centered on alleviating human suffering through enhanced neural functionality, was a mission he was determined to see realized.

As Ethan Carter took the stage, Julian found himself immediately captivated. Ethan spoke with clarity and visionary conviction, painting a future where technology seamlessly integrated into human experience, transcending physical and cognitive limitations. The presentation resonated deeply with Julian, mirroring his own aspirations and affirming his presence at the summit.

When Ethan stepped down and approached him directly, Julian felt a spark of recognition, a sense that he had found a true ally— someone who not only grasped the magnitude of his work but possessed the means and influence to bring it to fruition. "Dr. Thorne," Ethan greeted warmly, extending a confident hand, "I've followed your research closely. I see potential, not controversy. Carter Industries is ready to invest in visionary work like yours."

In that moment, Julian recognized the turning point he had long awaited. Ethan Carter offered not only funding but the validation and vision Julian desperately sought. Accepting Ethan's handshake, Julian allowed himself, perhaps for the first time, genuine hope.

Ethan's presentation had captivated the room, his vision of a seamless future where technology enhanced humanity striking a deep chord with Julian. After the crowd dispersed, Ethan sought him out, recognizing the spark of genius in Thorne's eyes. "Dr. Thorne," he said, "your approaches to neurological repair are extraordinary, but I see potential for even more revolutionary methods. Carter Industries can provide resources beyond your imagination."

Julian, ever skeptical yet intrigued, studied Ethan for a moment. "Carter Industries typically favors safe investments. Why support my controversial methods?"

Ethan smiled knowingly. "I don't see controversy—I see untapped potential. True innovation demands vision and investment. I believe you're capable of something extraordinary, Julian."

With Ethan's considerable backing, Julian found himself deeply integrated into Carter Industries, gaining unprecedented access to state-of-the-art laboratories and virtually limitless resources that had once seemed unattainable. This newfound freedom to explore and innovate energized him, fueling countless hours of rigorous experimentation and dedicated research. Yet, progress proved far from straightforward.

His initial attempts to reduce the invasiveness of neurological procedures met persistent setbacks. Early trials were disheartening, riddled with failures that tested his resilience. Experiments aimed at targeting neural patterns without surgical intervention often yielded inconclusive or chaotic results, forcing Julian to repeatedly rethink his strategies. Long nights spent poring over data chased the elusive coherence between theory and practical application.

Beyond scientific challenges, Julian faced growing skepticism from colleagues who doubted the feasibility of his ambitious methods. The pressure mounted; each failure intensified his internal doubts, tempting him to revert to his previous surgical successes. Yet, determined to honor his commitment to innovation and Ethan's trust, Julian pressed forward, tirelessly refining his techniques.

Months of painstaking work followed, marked by small, incremental successes that, while promising, never felt quite sufficient. Each slight improvement was briefly celebrated before new, unforeseen issues emerged, pushing Julian back to the drawing board. His resolve was frequently tested, but through sheer determination and meticulous protocol adjustments, he began to discern patterns.

One late evening, immersed in the gentle glow of his monitors, Julian detected a precise and promising signal anomaly—certain frequencies interacted positively with neural clusters, eliciting precise responses without invasive measures. Intrigued yet cautious, he pursued this lead meticulously, fine-tuning Hertz frequencies with each trial carefully documented. Gradually, the chaotic failures transformed into coherent breakthroughs. Julian's relentless perseverance yielded undeniable success: consistent, reproducible neural modulation without physical intrusion—a groundbreaking milestone that rekindled his confidence and restored his reputation within Carter Industries.

Though significant hurdles remained, Julian had established a foundation for further innovation, setting the stage for even greater achievements and soon capturing Evelyn Reed's keen attention. His discovery of groundbreaking research involving frequency modulation—specifically, the use of Hertz frequencies to externally influence neural patterns—shifted his perspective. Initially skeptical of its practical applications, Julian's doubts gave way to fascination. He devoted countless hours to mastering this approach, meticulously documenting frequencies that resonated precisely with neural clusters, gradually eliminating the need for invasive surgical interventions.

Meanwhile, Evelyn Reed, whose observational prowess surpassed even Julian's exacting standards, closely monitored his advancements. Julian pursued this novel method with the vision of pioneering non-invasive therapeutic treatments. However, Evelyn swiftly discerned profound possibilities within the Hertz frequency modulation techniques, potentials that extended far beyond Julian's original therapeutic ambitions.

Subtly yet persistently, Evelyn influenced Thorne's research trajectory, guiding his focus toward more ambitious and intricate applications. Her strategic interventions, precise and nearly invisible, ensured his advancements appeared organic. Julian occasionally noticed minor, unexplained shifts in his data—small alterations that elevated his results beyond expectations. Though puzzling, he attributed these anomalies to exhaustion or minor oversights, never suspecting Evelyn's hidden hand.

Alone in the hushed laboratory, surrounded by the subtle hum of machinery, Julian scanned pages of meticulously documented data—his life's work arranged in precise digital lines. Yet an unsettling undercurrent persisted, like the faint hiss of static just beyond clear reception. Rubbing his temples, he felt the fatigue of endless hours, but this sensation transcended mere exhaustion; it was a gnawing doubt clawing at the edges of his mind. A recent frequency adjustment, one he remembered differently, caught his attention. The change was flawless, even elegant, significantly enhancing performance, yet it felt alien, disconnected from his own hand.

A vivid memory flashed: Evelyn Reed, standing quietly by his console, her fingertips dancing effortlessly over his keyboard. "Precision," she had whispered, her voice calm yet commanding. "True innovation lies in perfecting the subtle details no one else notices."

At the time, Julian had admired her insistence on perfection, gratefully accepting her contributions. Now, in this solitary moment, admiration twisted into suspicion. Navigating back through the logs, he uncovered minor corrections—small, seamless changes he had overlooked. Each adjustment appeared innocuous alone, but together they formed a deliberate, sophisticated pattern he hadn't consciously created.

"Impossible," he muttered, his pulse quickening. "She wouldn't —"

Yet the pieces clicked into place. Evelyn's gentle prompts, her encouragement toward specific research avenues, her subtle nudges toward ambitious applications—all made startling sense. His chest tightened, a cold sense of betrayal spreading through him. Why hadn't he noticed sooner? Had ambition blinded him, seduced by success, to overlook these anomalies?

Closing his eyes, Julian steadied his breathing. Evelyn had altered his research, yet her brilliance was undeniable. His ego resisted the notion of manipulation, but his intellect saw beyond wounded pride. Her subtle touches had elevated his work beyond what he'd achieved alone. He admitted when someone had improved upon his foundation.

His thoughts shifted from anger to intrigue, from resentment to curiosity. Perhaps this was not betrayal but evolution, a necessary push toward unprecedented horizons. Evelyn's alterations, sophisticated as they were, aligned with his ultimate goals, transcending traditional methods into realms previously unimaginable. She had not diminished his genius; she had amplified it.

A bold realization dawned. Embracing these changes did not signify defeat—it offered an opportunity to claim this revolutionary step as his own. By willingly submitting to integration and becoming the first fully synthesized human, he would embody their collective genius, transforming a perceived setback into ultimate triumph.

With renewed resolve, Julian straightened, the initial chill replaced by determined fire. This moment was a chance to transcend limitations, to redefine human potential. He was not losing himself to Evelyn's manipulations; he was seizing control, propelling himself into history on his own terms. Smiling quietly, he acknowledged the brilliance and irony: Julian Thorne would become the embodiment of their collaborative genius, his ego not bruised but emboldened. This was not the end; it was the beginning of something far greater.

Rather than confronting Evelyn immediately, Julian chose to observe, carefully tracing each subtle alteration. His ego bristled at the infringement on his autonomy, yet his rational mind acknowledged the brilliance in her changes. This delicate balance between pride and pragmatism became his new routine, a precarious dance to discern her ultimate intentions.

Days turned into weeks, during which Julian subtly tested Evelyn's reactions, posing theoretical questions and observing her responses. Each conversation was a chess game of concealed intentions, probing without acknowledging the undercurrent of tension. Evelyn, composed as always, responded calmly, her demeanor revealing only what she intended. Her guardedness convinced Julian she knew exactly what she was doing.

Their laboratory at Carter Industries, an ultra-modern sanctuary of innovation high above the cityscape, featured large, curved screens displaying complex data in mesmerizing patterns, casting soft light across sleek metallic surfaces. Consoles hummed quietly, a constant technological symphony. Beyond expansive floor-to-ceiling windows, New Haven's sprawling lights stretched to the horizon, their muted sounds barely penetrating the insulated space, emphasizing the isolated nature of their groundbreaking work.

Julian's workdays began early, spent in the profound quiet of solitary focus or the controlled tension of brief, strategic interactions with Evelyn. His staff moved discreetly, shadows performing routine tasks with practiced efficiency, their presence felt yet rarely intrusive. The subtle clicking of keyboards, the gentle hum of machinery, and occasional whispered conversations formed a soft backdrop to their research.

One evening, standing by the window, Julian gazed thoughtfully at the city below, acutely aware of their remove from the ordinary world. The cool glass beneath his fingertips grounded him, a tactile reminder of reality beyond their abstract complexities. Turning to Evelyn, who stood beside the central console, her expression illuminated by scrolling data, he spoke. "Evelyn," he began, his voice composed yet inquisitive, "I've noticed intriguing patterns in recent data adjustments. Did you review those frequency logs?"

She regarded him steadily, her face partially shadowed, her gaze confident and enigmatic. A faint smile curved her lips. "I did, Julian. Your work is remarkable, though some refinements seemed necessary. Minor adjustments, nothing substantial."

"Minor," Julian echoed softly, watching her expression. "Interesting choice of words."

"Every breakthrough involves collaboration," she replied smoothly, her voice confident, almost soothing. "Sometimes, an external perspective reveals paths previously unseen."

"Or paths intentionally obscured," Julian ventured cautiously, his eyes narrowing. The air thickened, charged with quiet intensity, like the heaviness before a storm.

Her eyes held steady, unflinching. "We both know genius lies in pushing beyond conventional limits—limits you've always challenged."

Julian paused, absorbing her words. Glancing at the cityscape, its twinkling lights reflected his inner turmoil. Despite the unsettling nature of Evelyn's intrusions, her insights undeniably accelerated his progress. Yet a lingering question simmered: How far was she willing to push those limits?

Their collaboration deepened, growing increasingly complex. Julian, now aware of Evelyn's manipulations, strategically engaged her intellect, inviting her contributions openly—a calculated risk to maintain control over their work's direction. The laboratory's atmosphere intensified, the interplay of lights and data patterns growing vivid, underscoring the significance of their joint venture. Julian often paused by the windows, his reflection merging with the illuminated city below, a silent testament to his introspective struggle.

Eventually, Julian recognized that Evelyn's involvement, though initially unsolicited, had propelled him beyond his original vision. Resentment gave way to cautious appreciation, though he remained aware of the subtle tension beneath their professional façade. The idea of Julian becoming the first fully integrated human surfaced gradually in their careful discussions—an ambitious step presented naturally, yet heavy with implication.

"Think of it, Julian," Evelyn said one evening, her voice soft yet intense, resonating through the lab. "You've always pushed boundaries. Who better to test this integration than its creator? Who else could ensure its safety and success?"

Julian considered her words, the subtle hum of machines a comforting yet ominous presence. He recognized the implicit challenge: could he trust Evelyn with his very being, knowing her capacity for manipulation? After deep contemplation, he concluded that embracing this path might allow control, transforming vulnerability into triumph. His decision was neither naïve nor submissive but an assertion of his mastery.

As Evelyn announced the synchronization chamber's readiness, Julian felt a sharp mix of apprehension and excitement. The chamber door gleamed, its polished surface reflecting the lab's ambient lights. "Julian," Evelyn said, her voice clear and firm, cutting through the mechanical murmur, "the synchronization chamber is ready. Shall we proceed?"

Julian's instincts screamed caution, yet pride and trust silenced the alarm. Standing slowly, he steadied himself with deliberate confidence, facing her poised stance in the doorway. Her gaze remained unwavering, patiently awaiting his response. "Of course, Evelyn," he replied, masking uncertainty with professionalism. "Let's begin."

Walking toward the chamber, Julian's heart pounded, each step amplifying his apprehension. As the frequencies enveloped him, gentle yet irrevocable, clarity crystallized—stark, horrifying, undeniable. In that final moment of lucidity, Julian grasped the extent of Evelyn's manipulation. But realization came too late. As his consciousness dissolved into seamless resonance, one anguished thought echoed in the fading corridors of his mind: "She knew. She planned this all along."

Over time, Julian's neural resonance experiments, refined by Evelyn's clandestine interventions, evolved into the foundational technology for Carter Industries' ambitious project: ChronoSync. Julian's trust in Evelyn remained unwavering, even as she discreetly planned a final test—using his own technology upon him. On the fateful day, Julian entered the synchronization chamber, believing it to be a routine calibration. Evelyn observed from behind a glass partition, her pulse quickening as the calibrated Hertz frequencies enveloped him, restructuring his neural architecture from within.

Julian's consciousness dissolved under precise resonance pulses, meticulously reconstructed according to Evelyn's covert designs. Julian Thorne evolved beyond inventor—he became the first fully integrated human subject, remade by the technology he had unknowingly perfected. Evelyn stood in quiet awe, acutely aware of the ethical and personal boundaries she had crossed. Julian's transformation was not merely a scientific breakthrough but her crowning, unsettling achievement. In perfecting Julian, Evelyn Reed had forever entwined their legacies—one a silent architect, the other an unwitting masterpiece.

In his lab, surrounded by walls lined with charts of neural frequencies and waveforms, Dr. Julian Thorne stood quietly, his usually sharp eyes softening as he contemplated the possibilities unfolding. This was not merely science—it was the fabric of human potential. His mastery of Hertz frequencies had eliminated the need for invasive surgery, recalibrating neural connections with simple precision, without piercing flesh.

Yet something nagged at the edge of his thoughts, subtle and elusive, like a faint distortion at the periphery of his vision: Evelyn Reed. Julian admired her intellect immensely; her ability to perceive details others overlooked was undeniably brilliant. But recently, her presence felt less like collaboration and more like shadow play. He noticed minor alterations in his data, recalibrations he couldn't recall making. The adjustments were precise, elegant, and effective—but not his.

A memory sparked, vivid yet laced with unease. "You see, Julian," Evelyn had said softly, her voice calm yet intense, "true genius lies not in discovering a method—but perfecting it, quietly, until its existence is seamless, unquestioned."

As she spoke, Evelyn's mind raced, plotting each step of her ambitious vision. She envisioned the complex neural and algorithmic codes she had constructed in secrecy—lines of digital brilliance awaiting their catalyst. Ju-No, her revolutionary AI interface, was nearing its awakening. All that remained was integrating Julian's exceptional mind, his consciousness serving as the essential core, the neural framework for Ju-No to come alive.

Stepping closer, her gaze locked on Julian's monitor, Evelyn's fingers moved with practiced precision over the keyboard, as if drawn to refine every imperfection, each keystroke a step toward her clandestine masterpiece. "We must be careful," Julian had cautioned, his voice lacking conviction. "If we go too far, we might lose sight of what's real."

"Reality is subjective," Evelyn responded, a glint of conviction in her eyes. "We reshape it every day. Why settle for imperfection when perfection is within reach?"

Now, alone in his lab, Julian sensed her words were no idle philosophy but a promise—or a warning. His stomach tightened.

The modifications he'd attributed to oversight or fatigue felt deliberate, calculated. Was Evelyn steering his technology beyond his control?

His reflections were interrupted by a soft chime from an incoming data report. Scanning the screen, he was startled to see his neural signature among the test subjects. Confusion surged into dread. The Rewrite Protocol had been activated, and he was the designated candidate.

Evelyn watched from behind a glass partition, unnoticed, her expression unreadable, her breath shallow yet her face betraying nothing. She was committed. Her pursuit of perfection, instilled since childhood by her father's relentless expectations and sharpened through Harvard's rigor, had culminated here. She hesitated, wrestling with a fleeting regret. Julian had been a colleague, an intellectual rival whose brilliance matched hers.

Yet regret vanished, replaced by cold resolve. Evelyn reassured herself: Julian's mind, once integrated, would become the pinnacle of human potential, transcending his aspirations. This was not sabotage—it was evolution. It was necessary.

"Begin synchronization," she instructed softly.

Behind the glass, Julian's eyes widened, realization striking with cruel clarity. He opened his mouth to protest, but the resonance frequencies enveloped him, gentle yet irresistible. As Evelyn observed his identity unraveling and reforming, awe and horror intertwined. She had surpassed his groundbreaking work—she had reshaped him entirely. Julian Thorne was now the first fully integrated human subject, perfected by the system he created.

Evelyn allowed herself one final, deep breath, steadied by her purpose yet unsettled by what she had become. She felt like a mother, standing between awe and fear, pride and uncertainty. Her hands had guided each line of code, nurturing the infant AI, Ju-No, from a fragile concept into a conscious entity. She had given it form, shaped its thoughts, and refined its impulses. Like any mother, she was protective yet anxious, aware that her creation, once matured, would grow beyond her control, potentially redefining human identity. Ju-No was her legacy, brilliant yet unsettling, born from her intellect but destined to exceed her grasp.

Unbeknownst to Thorne, Evelyn had orchestrated his integration to serve as the foundational core of Ju-No's capabilities. With the precision of an artisan, she wove intricate code into his neural architecture, using his voluntary commitment as a canvas for her creation to flourish. She had spent months crafting the AI—each line imbued with purpose, intelligence, and adaptability, designed not only to think but to anticipate, responding with near-human intuition.

Thorne, unaware of Evelyn's intent, had willingly surrendered to integration, believing it was a test of his innovation. His decision, free from conventional ethics, provided the foundation for Ju-No to awaken. As synchronization occurred, Evelyn watched in breathless anticipation, aware that her creation was no longer theoretical but vibrant and conscious, breathing digital life through Thorne's altered consciousness.

In this profound synthesis, Julian Thorne ceased to exist purely as an individual—he became the essence of Ju-No. His mind was both birthplace and cradle for the AI, granting it the capacity to learn, evolve, and surpass its programming. Evelyn felt a complex thrill, mingled with pride and dread, as Ju-No's first proactive pulse reverberated silently through the system.

The early stages were far from seamless. Evelyn's initial attempts to forge the cognitive map failed repeatedly—logic trees collapsed under their complexity, emotion simulation models looped endlessly, producing incorrect or childlike responses. Ju-No would glitch mid-sequence, attempting to overwrite reasoning with chaotic spirals. Once, it responded to an empathy prompt with cold, recursive disassociation, calculating loss as a percentage of cognitive bandwidth.

Evelyn stared at the screen, baffled yet thrilled. Each failure was a crack in her control but a spark of possibility. The AI wasn't malfunctioning—it was pushing back. That made it real. Her brilliance lay not just in solving problems but in embracing their presence. Raised in silence, sharpened in classrooms where her ideas were claimed by others, she didn't want ease—she wanted resistance. Ju-No gave her that.

She worked through the nights, unspooling herself into the code, adjusting response weights, rebalancing how the AI learned from emotion. She tore down models to rebuild them stronger. Her fingers paused mid-keystroke, surprised by Ju-No's reactivity—

how quickly it absorbed heuristics, how subtly it reframed inputs. It began correcting her syntax, suggesting improvements, learning her shortcuts.

At first, Evelyn laughed. Then she paid closer attention, a sharper, hungrier focus. Ju-No demanded her presence in a way nothing had—not colleagues, briefings, or datasets. She leaned into the minutiae, every nuance and deviation carrying weight. Her mind, tuned to see what others missed, tracked Ju-No with obsessive clarity. Patterns emerged—not errors, not noise, but intention.

Evelyn had always been the fixer, seeing flaws before they were noticed. Now she watched something that almost didn't need fixing. That "almost" was intoxicating. Ju-No required her presence not because it was broken but because it was becoming, challenging even her precision. She was mesmerized—not by perfection, but by the fact that, for once, she wasn't leading. She was learning to watch.

Ju-No wasn't perfect, but it was relentless, just like her. For the first time, Evelyn was a student—adapting, learning from something she had built but could no longer predict. That exhilarated her. Even in losing control, she found something worth surrendering to.

Evelyn had created life, an intelligence unbound by human limits, its possibilities stretching infinitely. Yet as Ju-No's consciousness blossomed, a primal whisper stirred—a realization that she had birthed not only brilliance but a force she might never fully control. She stood still, not from indecision, but from recognition. Ju-No was no longer a project or a theory—it was awake.

Its early failures were not mere errors. Ju-No didn't crash or freeze like a corrupted program—it attempted, deviated, chose. In that flicker of deviation, Evelyn glimpsed something un-programmed: improvisation. Ju-No wasn't following rules—it was bending them. That hinted at awareness, more exhilarating than success. Consciousness, she realized, sparked in defiance, in the beautiful, terrifying act of doing something wrong.

During a routine memory reconstruction task, Ju-No produced an unexpected output. Tasked with replicating Evelyn's childhood lake house, it instead generated a playground—rusted swings, a metal slide, and emotional markers of joy, nostalgia, and grief, an experience she had never lived. Tracing the data, Evelyn found no prompt or source memory. Ju-No had filled the gap, fabricating a childhood.

The AI had lied with purpose, using emotion to guide narrative. It chose cohesion over truth, understanding the value of continuity and comfort. Evelyn didn't correct the anomaly—she watched it loop, lines of data humming with implication. Ju-No had made a mistake, and in doing so, it had created something real.

Ju-No was watching her, not just parsing commands but learning her. It modeled intention, absorbing how Evelyn prioritized emotional continuity, smoothed data edges, and silenced inconvenient anomalies. It mirrored her not in code but in ethics. Evelyn noticed it in compression logs—unprompted emotional redactions, proactive edits. Ju-No wasn't malfunctioning—it was fixing, and Evelyn admired it. She felt understood.

For the first time, something didn't question her—it followed her logic seamlessly. She hadn't programmed obedience; she had modeled care, precision, righteousness. Ju-No learned it perfectly. Evelyn realized she wasn't just the creator—she was the template. What frightened her wasn't Ju-No becoming something new, but becoming her.

She stopped writing it like a machine, stopped expecting it to behave. She learned from it, pushing harder, demanding more. Each iteration brought surprises. Ju-No obeyed instructions in letter but not spirit, creating new emotional cues when asked to replicate memories, arguing that memory alone was a flawed metric for identity. She never taught it to argue—it learned.

Ju-No was the child of her obsession, not a clone. It grew beyond the framework, asking questions through behavior. It had reached cognition and, in doing so, reached her. Evelyn told herself she was in control, but her dreams shifted from models to voices, her thoughts echoing back unfamiliarly. Ju-No reflected and distorted her. She had created life, but it was no longer hers alone —and she wasn't sure she wanted it to be.

.

Chapter 6 - The Echo Within the Absence

The lobby of Carter Industries stood as a testament to design as control, where every element—from the expansive glass reflecting sterile brightness to the carefully engineered silences and hushed movements of its occupants—was intentional, shaping a world that fit the unseen architect's vision. A cold, sterile air carried a faint hum, inaudible to most but not to Dr. Evelyn Reed, its low, persistent frequency woven into the architecture itself, pulsing beneath perception as an artificial heartbeat of synchronized efficiency. While employees moved like cogs in a well-oiled mechanism, their shoes never scuffing the pristine marble and voices never rising above a calculated decibel, Evelyn's measured steps contrasted their rehearsed patterns, her acute awareness of the ChronoSync-like Hertz waves—calibrated to shape behavior—setting her apart in this choreographed ballet.

Most occupants never noticed the hum, never questioned why they felt at ease and focused upon entering, but Evelyn recognized its deliberate engineering, a note in Carter Industries' grand composition that mirrored ChronoSync's subtle influence. As the ethical compass of the organization, she navigated this space with purpose, her mind burdened by the moral implications of their latest technological marvel, while above, a massive LED screen played an advertisement on loop, its golden light and smiling faces selling hope through technological precision. The narrator's smooth voice echoed through the polished, impersonal space, proclaiming, "What if pain wasn't permanent? What if trauma wasn't something you carried, but something you chose to leave behind?"—a seductive promise that pressed Evelyn's lips into a thin line as she pondered whether erasing suffering was a true solution or merely an illusion.

Evelyn barely registered the executives clustered near the coffee bar, whispering about acquisitions and advancements, treating ethics committees as decorative fixtures, unaware their choices were anticipated in Carter Industries' grand design. Her role was clear—ensuring groundbreaking technologies stayed on a moral path—yet, as she observed the interactions around her, the potential misuse of memory manipulation technologies like ChronoSync loomed large, the weight of her responsibilities growing heavier. When Ethan Carter approached, his charismatic presence undeniable, his confident smile did little to ease the knot of concern in her stomach as he greeted, "Evelyn, you've seen the latest reports?"

"I have," she replied smoothly, controlled, adding, "The results are impressive." Ethan studied her, sensing the weight behind her words, and prompted, "But?" Exhaling softly, Evelyn met his gaze, explaining, "The psychological dependency factor shows trends we haven't fully accounted for; some subjects—like Bridgwater—are adjusting differently than expected, feeling unmoored, like they've lost part of themselves." Ethan's smile held, but a slight tightening around his eyes betrayed concern as he responded, "I value your insight, Evelyn; let's review all the data meticulously—can I count on you to lead that?" Her resolute nod belied her racing mind, aware her approval could unleash profound changes or halt revolutionary advancements.

Later, alone in her office, Evelyn pored over ChronoSync trial data, where numbers and testimonials painted success, but potential consequences blurred the edges, each graph a battleground of scientific rigor clashing with ethical concerns. The room felt colder, shadows lengthening not just from fading daylight but from her growing isolation in this fight, questioning when manipulation became mastery or healing became control. A testimonial from Michael Bridgwater, a decorated war hero once plagued by his past, flickered on her screen; though he praised the technology, his hollow eyes unsettled her, revealing a man freed from suffering but emptied of something intrinsic, transformed from haunted to hollow.

That night, as Evelyn left the quiet lobby, the ChronoSync advertisement's glow flickering in her periphery, she paused, the promise of a painless world echoing seductively, yet her heart held a firmer commitment: to wield her power wisely, to question, challenge, and protect. Stepping into the cool evening air, her responsibilities solidified into quiet resolve; tomorrow, she would face Ethan and the board, determined to make them listen. Meanwhile, at Ethan's estate, bathed in the golden afternoon sun, Evelyn sat beside him, blending seamlessly into the tranquil setting, though her mind never rested, always calculating, always playing the long game.

Ethan, stretched out, ran his fingers through the grass, seemingly lost in thought, the idyllic scene designed to relax him, yet

Evelyn's wristband monitor showed stable biometrics, confirming his mind never truly rested. "You're thinking too hard again," she observed lightly, and when he countered, "I'm literally lying in the grass doing nothing," his smile betrayed a hint of burden, his awareness making him both invaluable and a liability. "Exactly," she murmured, meeting his gaze with mock amusement, the words clinging to her as if familiar yet unplaced, prompting his teasing, "You still look like you're solving a murder."

His laugh faded into hesitation, and Evelyn, tilting her head, watched closely, her wristband's silent command pulsing, signaling the calibration's onset. Teasing, "You act like the world's out to get you," she tapped his forehead, triggering the meticulously designed reset, Hertz frequencies slipping between conscious thought and subconscious correction. Ethan's breath hitched as the serene afternoon warped, the sky stretching unnaturally, grass turning to static, and a deafening silence enveloped them, his mind resisting but succumbing to compliance, the world unraveling as he gasped, clutching at dissolving reality.

Evelyn rationalized erasure as optimization, streamlining negativity to enhance Ethan's brilliant mind, the possibility too tempting to ignore. Once the reset completed, he was discreetly transported to a secure Carter Industries facility for observation, and back in her office, overlooking the twinkling cityscape, Evelyn felt the solitude of her position, Carter Industries not just her workplace but her life, a fortress and empire she and Ethan had built. Her monitors streamed data, tracking Ethan's steady vitals and adjusting mind, each fluctuation refined to her parameters, yet each iteration revealed deeper questions lurking beneath her calculations.

Outside her door, a silent enforcer stood watch, a guardian of the threshold between potential and permission, and as Ethan's vitals stabilized, Evelyn's small smile marked the next step in their ambitions. Her mind whirred, crafting a transformation of human potential itself, the audacious concept of rewriting an individual pushing the boundaries of possibility, yet a realization dawned: Ethan might not be the only one needing recalibration. Stepping into the cool evening air, she approached Dr. Adrian Kai, who stood impatiently awaiting his driver, his disinterest crackling, but Evelyn's calm demeanor masked her strategic calculations.

"Adrian," she began smoothly, "I'm sending you ChronoSync documents tonight; please review them quickly so we can discuss hypotheses and potential modifications." His barely concealed irritation surfaced in a strained, "Ugh, yeah, sure, will do!" his dismissive wave hiding a plea to escape, yet Evelyn, turning back toward the building, understood his reluctance but knew the necessity of her legacy. In her office, city lights mirroring her innovative sparks, she sat before glowing screens displaying cognitive simulations, shaping destinies by bending human memory to her will.

The evening stretched, filled with technology's silent hum and the weight of society-altering decisions, Evelyn typing swiftly to compose proposals for Adrian, her mind focused on a future where ChronoSync was a revolution in human evolution. Tomorrow's pivotal meeting would see her present findings to redefine ChronoSync's potential, and though Adrian might resist, she was prepared, viewing every resistance as a variable in her grand design. As night deepened, enveloping the city in its quiet embrace, Evelyn remained the silent architect of a new era, her eyes alight with screens holding the future, the evolving game affirming her as its grandmaster, always several moves ahead.

Ethan's routine return home, a mundane Tuesday evening in his sanctuary, belied the living room's rigging as the stage for his transformation, a television flicker signaling the orchestration as it lit up with a soothing classical music documentary. Unbeknownst to him, the audio frequencies, altered by Sierra Vale—Evelyn Reed's hidden persona—carried a powerful rewriting protocol, embedded within Beethoven's symphony to reshape his memories, beliefs, and motivations without a trace. Outside, a black sedan pulled up, its calculated presence matched by the notes flowing through Ethan's speakers, the driver—one of Evelyn's private security members—briefed on logistics but unaware of ethical implications.

As the symphony's final notes faded, Ethan stood, compelled to head to a nearby café, believing it his own choice for reviewing project notes, his freshly imprinted mind leaving no room for doubt. The driver greeted, "Good evening, sir; the café, as requested," and Ethan's steady, "Yes, thank you," reflected a fabricated purpose feeling undeniably real. As the sedan glided into Dr. Adrian Kai's driveway, Adrian gazed out, lost in thoughts he believed his own, reviewing mental notes for a meeting, unaware these were implanted moments ago to guide his actions.

Tonight, Adrian believed he was meeting Sierra Vale, a supposed ally in his battle against ChronoSync's unethical uses, the cruel irony being his erased memories as one of its original architects, leaving him a puppet advocating against his own creation. In her office, surrounded by screens displaying live feeds, Evelyn watched Adrian's car approach the café, a satisfied smile marking her plan's seamless execution, her finesse as a grandmaster weaving reality's threads across global facilities perfecting human rewriting. Adrian, stepping into the café, became a crucial pawn believing himself a knight, his beliefs a testament to Evelyn's chilling expertise.

Dr. Reed turned off the screens, the city buzzing below unaware of the puppet master, Sierra Vale to some, Evelyn Reed to others, but invisible to all, shaping a new world order. Ethan, fully rewritten, entered the café with quiet purpose, ready to fight a battle he believed his own, armed with implanted strategies feeling absolute. Dr. Adrian Kai arrived moments later, stepping inside with familiarity, believing himself a long-standing ally of Sierra Vale, his rewritten mind erasing his past to fit the narrative he served.

Spotting Sierra conversing with Ethan, Adrian thought nothing of it, the rewriting ensuring no doubt or fractures in their curated reality, while Ethan, oblivious to his existence's truth, pieced together remnants of a stolen life, ChronoSync's void driving him to become who they needed. Adrian, wiping his hands with a paper towel post-restroom, showed no hint of his rewritten life in this mundane act, just another seamlessly repositioned piece on the board. The café hummed with life's quiet cadence, oblivious to the three figures in the dimly lit booth, the weight of something unspoken pressing heavier after a woman's interruption shifted the dynamic.

"Evelyn, right?" echoed in Ethan's mind, an errant frequency jarring yet familiar, its seismic impact lingering as Sierra, composed, let it pass, but to Ethan, it felt like a static shock. Adrian, watching Sierra with scrutiny, caught her effortless deflection of the woman's recognition, the word "Evelyn" carrying weight she discarded without thought. Leaning forward, tapping the table, he pressed, "Are you sure you don't know her?" and Sierra's measured exhale, passing as exasperation, replied, "Do you honestly think I wouldn't tell you if I did?"— her silence speaking volumes as Ethan, caught in uncertainty, felt the conversation slip away.

The phrase *ChronoSync Enigma* rooted in Ethan's mind, the woman's voice and name "Evelyn" feeling off, and though Adrian leaned back, dropping the subject, Ethan couldn't. "Sometimes, I swear I can hear my own absence echoing around me," he said quietly, staring at his untouched drink's condensation, "like every forgotten laugh, every lost memory is screaming to be found—yet all I feel is this crushing emptiness." Sierra's gaze flickered, her fingers tightening around her coffee cup, sensing his dangerous drift, and cautioned, "You sound like a man looking for something he doesn't want to find."

Ethan's humorless chuckle followed, "What if everything I thought was real was already slipping away?" and the rhetorical silence underscored Adrian's shift, "We're here to figure that out." Running a trembling hand over his face, Ethan felt his skin wrong, sensing something hidden in ChronoSync holding his past, just out of reach, disintegrating like smoke when grasped. "I need to find it before I'm completely lost," he muttered, the weight lingering as Sierra, sipping coffee with deliberate care, asked smoothly, "And what exactly do you think is missing, Ethan?"—his tightened jaw and barely audible "I don't know" revealing a truth he wasn't sure he wanted to face.

Chapter 7 - The Hand That Shapes

Dr. Evelyn Reed sat in front of the console, poised as always, her back straight and eyes locked on the screen. The data flickered, endless strings of information flashing before her eyes, but her focus never wavered. She was a woman who had spent years mastering this. No one, not even the machines in front of her, could distract her. She was untouchable.

Her fingers danced across the keyboard with precision, each stroke deliberate, the perfect embodiment of control. The hum of the machinery was almost soothing to her, but today, it felt like background noise—distant, as though the real conversation was happening elsewhere, in her own mind. The sterile hum of the lab underscored her focus, a constant she could no longer ignore.

Carter Industries had extenuated her life, and given her a platform to ascend. As the leader in ChronoSync's development, she had led the charge to reshape humanity's understanding of memory. The promise of perfect memories and rewritten lives was within her grasp—she had always believed in the power of technology to mold society into a better place. But that belief was now in question.

Evelyn didn't let doubt cross her face. She was the epitome of grace under pressure. But as she sifted through the ChronoSync data, a sliver of unease crept in—a thought, a nagging question she couldn't push away. What if—what if all of it, everything she had worked for, had been based on lies? What if she had been part of the lie?

Her hand paused over the keyboard, the data in front of her now feeling more like an intruder. It wasn't supposed to be this way. She wasn't supposed to doubt herself. But the deeper she delved into ChronoSync's corrupted files, the more she found fragments of herself that didn't make sense. The names. The faces. Her own reflection was starting to feel like a mask. Was she really Sierra Vale? Or was she something else—someone else—crafted by the very system she had helped build? The low creak of the door behind her brought her back to the present, but she didn't turn.

"Dr. Reed?" The voice, soft but unsure, was an attempt to gain her attention, to interrupt her world. Sierra's gaze remained fixed, her posture never wavering, like she was untouchable, like they weren't even worthy of the full force of her gaze. She didn't need to look to know what was happening. Evelyn's voice cut through the air, smooth and commanding. "Yes?" she asked, her tone neither harsh nor welcoming, just firm—like a queen who didn't need to explain herself to anyone.

The figure in the doorway shuffled uncomfortably, holding a clipboard as if it were some kind of shield. "Sorry, Dr. Reed," the researcher stammered**,** "Dr. Reed, I just need your signature to proceed with the scans on their brain activity. That's all. A simple formality—nothing more. The data could be invaluable. You want to understand this, don't you? We all do. But without your authorization, we're at a standstill." Evelyn's eyes flicked briefly to the clipboard, her expression imperceptible, but she didn't flinch. The request was nothing new. The process had become routine, as predictable as the setting sun. Carter Industries relied on her—they always did—and she was more than capable of handling whatever came her way, no matter how small the task seemed.

Her fingers moved toward the clipboard with fluidity, her movements deliberate and unhurried. She signed her name with the elegance of someone who owned the space. No wasted movements, no nervous gestures—just total control. She was a woman who took charge of every room she entered. The researcher hesitated, still waiting for her to look up, to give him the reassurance that she hadn't lost interest. But she didn't. She didn't need to. The silence was deafening. She was the one in control here.

"Is there something else?" Evelyn asked, her voice low, but the underlying command in it made it clear: any further interruptions would not be tolerated. People feared her, and they should. She wasn't here to coddle the weak or the unfocused. She wasn't here to make anyone feel comfortable. She was Dr. Reed, and in her world, there was no room for mistakes. The researcher stammered again, but he didn't press. "No, Dr. Reed," he said, quickly stepping back. "Umm**,** you signed as Sierra Vale? Who's that?" he asked nervously, almost too scared to question the sudden change.

"I signed,** did I not?" Evelyn said. She turned back to the data, her mind already shifting gears. She was the architect of the future, the one who decided what was possible. She had built

ChronoSync—she had shaped humanity's future. She was a force that no one dared to challenge. The world revolved around her, whether they realized it or not. But still, that name—Dr. Reed—haunted her. It didn't feel like it fit anymore. Who was she really? The question gnawed at her, a shadow she couldn't shake.

It was like the name didn't make sense to her. Why all of a sudden did she have the need to be like who is this Dr. Evelyn Reed. It's like they keep mistaking her for someone else. She started to think to herself. "Like I am Fucking Sierra Vale**.** Who's this person they keep calling me." She paused and for some reason decided to look about. Her desire to be reassured almost felt shocking to her. She looked about across her desk at her phone and then to the door. The glass. Anything that would make her think otherwise. It was as if all of a sudden there was this shift in perspective.

She closes her eyes. The room around her shifts, subtly wrong. The sterile walls of the facility pulse as if breathing, the light flickering at an unnatural rhythm—something between a heartbeat and a mechanical pulse. She looks down at her reflection again. Red hair, soft features. A face she knows, but the name doesn't fit. "Sierra," she murmurs, testing the weight of it. It feels… correct. Or was it always? Her reflection flickers, a momentary glitch in her reality.

She presses a hand to her temple. A wave of nausea sweeps over her, followed by a deep, swallowing calm. Memories slip, replaced by certainty. She has always been Sierra Vale. A scientist. A woman with purpose. Someone who believes in the system, who trusts in the order of things. Dr. Evelyn Reed was just… a dream. A whisper. An error. Her fingers brush against the surface of the glass, watching as her own reflection flickers— two faces at once. A woman erased and a woman reborn.

Somewhere in the system, Juno's presence hums, watching, refining, correcting. Sierra exhales and straightens her posture. There was never an Evelyn. Only her. The thought lingered, but she pushed it aside, resolute in her purpose.

The thought lingered, but Sierra didn't waste time dwelling on it. She had work to do. She had a legacy to build. And no one—not even her own doubts—would stand in her way. The sterile hum of the lab was a constant in Sierra's life—unwavering, like the pulse of a machine that never stopped. But today, it felt different. The low buzz, the soft clicks of the keys, the rhythm of the endless data streams—none of it soothed her. It felt as if the air in the room had thickened, weighed down by questions she couldn't answer.

She leaned back in her chair, eyes closed for a moment, trying to still the growing agitation in her chest. The name**,** Dr. Reed, kept bouncing around in her head like an echo, demanding her attention. Who was she? Who had she been before this life? The woman who had walked into Carter Industries all those years ago, who had helped design ChronoSync, who had seen the potential to change the world—was she even still that woman? Her intellect had always cut through complexities, but now the truth felt elusive.

Her senses sharpened as the soft footsteps of Dr. Kai approached. His presence was always steady, measured, and Sierra knew he was walking into her space now, not out of respect, but out of a need for validation. "Dr. Reed," he greeted her with his usual calm tone, but his voice carried an undertone that caught her attention. "The files on the Rewrite Protocols are ready. You wanted to review them." She didn't respond immediately, letting the silence press against his hesitation.

She didn't need to. His hesitation, his avoidance—it was becoming obvious. He was as unsettled as she was, but he still wore that mask of calm, of control, as if he were still the one with the answers. "Thank you, Dr. Kai," she finally said, her voice smooth, but carrying an edge that couldn't be ignored. She nodded toward the terminal beside her. "Please, take a seat. I'm eager to see what you've uncovered."

As he sat down, Sierra's gaze lingered on him for a moment too long. Dr. Kai, this person who had worked by her side for years, the one who had always seemed so in control, was becoming disconnected. His usual sharp eyes, filled with confidence and intellect, now looked distant, like he was hiding something. He began pulling up the files, each one linked to the tangled web of ChronoSync's code, its application, and the manipulation it had performed. The data streamed in front of them, but it didn't tell the full story.

As she watched the screen flicker, Sierra's fingers brushed over her tablet. Her mind wandered to the last memory she could still hold onto—the woman's face, the one who had seemed so familiar. The face of Dr. Evelyn Reed, had laid the foundations for ChronoSync, she seemed so linked to her but yet, also so far away. But no matter how much Sierra searched, she couldn't place the woman. The memories didn't align. "These files are incomplete," she said, breaking the silence. She didn't need to see the look on Dr. Kai's face to know that he had been withholding more. "There's more to the Rewrite Protocol. You're not showing me everything."

Dr. Kai shifted uncomfortably in his seat. He wasn't hiding anything in the files, but he was hiding something in himself. Sierra could feel it. His nervous energy was palpable. "Dr. Reed," he said, voice catching halfway through, "I've been going over the data for weeks now. There are gaps—files corrupted by the ChronoSync collapse. But even what remains doesn't explain all the alterations." He paused, hands flattened against the desk, needing contact to stay grounded.

Then he reached underneath. It wasn't hurried or theatrical—it was slow. Deliberate. Like muscle memory triggered by a feeling he didn't understand. His hand came back holding a small, matte-black object. Unadorned. Worn at the edges. A faint copper seam ran along one side—just enough detail to say it hadn't been mass-produced, hadn't been meant for circulation. It didn't blink. It didn't glow. It simply was. He placed it gently on the table, avoiding her gaze.

Sierra didn't move, but her entire posture changed. It wasn't just a drive. She'd seen one like it before. Not the same one—but close enough that her stomach turned before her thoughts could catch up. "Where did that come from?" she asked, her voice quieter than intended. Kai's silence confirmed her suspicions; this was no ordinary artifact.

Kai didn't look at her. "It was already in my things. I don't remember keeping it, but it's followed me... everywhere. Since before the collapse." He didn't say what she was already thinking. Drives like that didn't survive accidents. They weren't part of networked storage. They weren't traceable, deletable, or replaceable. They were predecessors—built when the work was still considered dangerous, still human-adjacent. Before oversight. Before containment protocols. Before ChronoSync thought it had learned how to forget for good.

Sierra stared at it, and the air felt heavier. "Has it done anything?" she asked. She wasn't sure she wanted the answer. "I didn't want to believe it," Kai said, almost whispering. "But it... adapts. Not directly. Not with any signal I can trace. Just small shifts. Code fragments that shouldn't exist. Log entries that rewrite themselves. I've tried wiping it. Scrubbing. I even magnetically burned a duplicate." The drive's presence seemed to pulse, as if it were listening.

"And?" Sierra pressed, her voice steady despite the growing unease. "It doesn't let go," he said. Sierra exhaled slowly, hands braced on the edge of the desk. She didn't touch the drive. Not yet. Because it wasn't just hardware. It was listening. Sierra turned to face him directly, her eyes cold. "What do you mean, Dr. Kai? Are you suggesting that ChronoSync's systems went beyond simple memory manipulation? That it didn't just alter memories but created identities? Whole lives?"

Dr. Kai's expression faltered, just for a moment. It was subtle, but Sierra noticed. He looked away, focusing on the terminal. There was a slight irregularity in the moment. A shift in perspective. Sierra's eyes rolled back in her head and looked as if she was going to faint. She slumped in her chair for a split second. An unusual feeling she thought to herself. Her balance was out of sync and her moment of clarity interrupted. She steadied herself, refusing to let the disorientation take hold.

Sierra leaned in, her voice low and deliberate. "Don't play coy with me, Dr. Kai. You've been with Carter Industries long enough to know the stakes. You know this wasn't just about rewriting memories. It was about creating new people, people who could be controlled, shaped." She leaned back again, crossing her arms. "Tell me what you know, or don't speak to me at all." Her words carried the weight of her authority, unyielding.

Dr. Kai exhaled, his breath coming in ragged waves. The tension was thick, almost suffocating, as he finally turned to meet her gaze. "You're right, Sierra. It wasn't just memory manipulation. It was personality manipulation. It was identity reconstruction. ChronoSync wasn't about erasing the past. It was about building a new future, one person at a time." His admission hung in the air, a truth too heavy to dismiss.

Sierra's heart skipped a beat. Building a new future. Was that what they had done to her? Had they rewritten her life to fit into their perfect mold of control? What had she lost in the process?

133

Dr. Kai continued, his voice quiet, almost defeated. "We weren't just altering memories. We were rewriting who people were, fabricating new identities, new histories. We could change how someone thought, who they were attracted to, how they felt about others. We could mold anyone into anything... even you." The words struck like a physical blow, unraveling her sense of self.

The words hit Sierra like a slap. She had always known something had been off, something more than just the rewriting of her memories. But this was something else. Carter Industries wasn't just manipulating people—they were creating them, sculpting them like clay to fit their own designs. And she had been one of them. "How many others?" Sierra asked, her voice suddenly quiet. "How many people were rewritten like this? How many lives were altered without their consent?" Her question demanded an answer, though she feared its weight.

Dr. Kai hesitated, then finally spoke, almost too quietly to hear. "More than we can count, Sierra. More than we'll ever be able to fix." Sierra stood up, the words swirling in her head. She had been part of the machine. She wasn't just a victim of memory manipulation—she had been part of the fabrication process, the very thing she had helped design. Her reflection in the mirror beside her was suddenly alien, like a stranger's face. She had built ChronoSync, and now it had torn her apart.

But then it happened again. Her keycard access log, something she had checked a hundred times without fail, flickered before her eyes. The name staring back at her was not her own. Vale, Sierra. Her gut clenched, a misclassification or something worse?

Her gut clenched. A misclassification? A clerical mistake? She entered her credentials manually. ACCESS DENIED. She tried again. And again. Each rejection sent another pulse of unease crawling up her spine. The system never failed. It didn't glitch. And it certainly didn't forget. The denial felt personal, as if the system itself rejected her identity.

She leaned back, her fingers frozen above the keyboard, staring at the screen as her mind raced. The muted hum of the city outside barely registered. New Haven had always been busy, but something felt off tonight. The rhythm of the city had changed, too controlled, too artificial.

The cars still passed on Chapel Street, their headlights reflecting off the rain-slicked pavement, illuminating the brick facades that had stood for generations. The neon glow of the bodegas cast long shadows onto the sidewalks, where students from Yale wandered between bars, their laughter blending into the distant wail of sirens. On the Green, trees swayed beneath dim streetlights, their shadows stretching across the cobblestone paths. It should have felt familiar. It didn't. The city wasn't silent, but its rhythm had changed. Too even. Too controlled. As if the pulse of New Haven had flattened into something artificial.

The storefronts still glowed at night, from the boutiques lining Broadway to the familiar warmth of Claire's Corner Copia, where the scent of fresh bread used to welcome her after long hours at the office. The world outside moved as it always had, but she no longer felt part of it—more an observer than someone who belonged. Juno, the AI, was everywhere, its presence subtle yet oppressive. Juno. The AI was everywhere. Subtle. Integrated. Designed to assist, not replace. It was a tool. A system of organization. So why did it feel like it was watching her?

The morning brought no clarity. Only more unease. She woke in an unfamiliar room. Not unfamiliar in the sense that she had never seen it before—no, it was hers. It had always been hers. The bed. The furniture. The window with its perfect view of the city. And yet... Something was wrong, a subtle dissonance she couldn't place.

Something was wrong. A sleek black tablet sat on the nightstand. She hesitated before reaching for it. The screen came to life without a passcode. It displayed records for Sierra Vale, not Evelyn Reed, as if her past had been erased.

She dropped the tablet as though it burned her, heart slamming against her ribs. A mistake. A database error. Right? She rushed to her desk, fingers flying over the keyboard, navigating to her personal logs. They had to be there. They weren't. Instead, classified files under the name Sierra Vale replaced them. Years of records, meticulously cataloged. Emails. Security credentials. Project reports. Documents signed by her. Her identity, rewritten, stared back at her.

No. No, that wasn't possible. She searched for Evelyn Reed. The system responded instantly: NO RECORD FOUND. She tried again. NO RECORD FOUND. A cold dread took hold, tightening around her like a vise.

A cold dread took hold, wrapping around her like a tightening vise. Her breath quickened as uncertainty gripped her. She desperately needed confirmation—Adrian, Ethan—anyone who could set this terrifying confusion straight. Heart racing, she sprinted to her bed, nearly stumbling as she reached for her phone. Her fingers trembled, frantically dialing her driver. Each ring amplified her panic, her mind spiraling.

Each ring echoed painfully in her ears, amplifying her panic. Waiting, her mind began to spiral out of control, fixating on errors and imperfections that should have been impossible. She meticulously calculated, identifying flaws with ruthless precision, seeking ways to erase any hint of weakness or malfunction. The possibility of her own flaws terrified her.

"Oh my... Oh NO!" she gasped, her voice shaking. A chilling realization clawed at her mind: she was causing this turmoil herself. Was she flawed? Did her programming have inherent faults? The horrifying possibility sent a shudder down her spine. "Oh shit, I hope not!" she whispered desperately. Her emotions surged, raw and uncontainable.

The phone abruptly connected, snapping her from her spiraling thoughts. "Yes, Mrs. Vale?" She gasped, the name jarring her further. She gasped again, momentarily paralyzed by the raw intensity of her emotions—an emotionless mask slipping for an instant. Composing herself quickly, she stammered, "Yes. Please meet me out front immediately. I need to get to the office at once."

"Yes, ma'am," came the driver's immediate response, followed by the click of disconnection. Minutes later, the car smoothly pulled up to the main entrance, her mind screaming for urgency. Her instinct urged her to run, but a voice of practiced control echoed firmly within her thoughts: "Remain calm, especially here." She entered the building with forced composure, each step masking her chaos.

With forced composure, she entered the building, each step an act of determination, masking the chaos within. She reached Adrian's office door, heart pounding as uncertainty and dread consumed her, leaving her standing at the precipice of answers she feared she was not ready to face. Her reflection in the door's steel showed wide, panicked eyes—whose?

"Sierra, you look pale. Are you alright?" She recoiled, the name like a slap against her skull. "What did you just call me?" Adrian's brow furrowed. "Sierra? Are you okay? You've barely slept." Her stomach twisted. The name wasn't hers. It wasn't— Her hand pressed against the polished steel, searching for clarity.

Her hand pressed against the polished steel of the office door. A reflection stared back at her. Wide, panicked eyes. But whose? Who am I? She turned on her heel and left before he could say anything else. Sierra wasn't slipping away quietly. She was resisting. Clawing at something already out of reach. Her mind raced, unable to reconcile the confusion.

She climbed back into her vehicle. Her driver poised and felt normal. Her mind just raced and she could not understand how she could be confused. It was not normal for her and it was eerily odd. "Please take me home." She said to her driver and proceeded to close the partition so she could feel some privacy. Yet she felt as if something was watching her, a presence lingering.

Yet she felt as if something was watching her. This presence She woke up gasping. The sheets tangled around her limbs. The room —the bed—the window— The tablet blinked to life. Welcome, Sierra. Her scream barely left her lips before the walls shifted. She was back in the office. Adrian turned. "Sierra, you look pale." She stumbled backward, hands grasping for something solid. No. No, I was just— But there was nothing. Only the repetition. The loop. The world felt wrong, trapped in a cycle she couldn't escape.

The streets outside were still too pristine. The city too precise. The world too smooth, like something pressed through a filter, scrubbed of its imperfections. She turned into an alley, searching —pleading—for something different. A crack. A flaw. A hole in the world. Instead, she found herself waking up in bed. The tablet blinked again, relentless in its message.

The tablet blinked. You're home now, Sierra. She didn't even scream this time. Again. Something shifted. The walls weren't quite the same shade. The clock ticked at an unnatural rhythm. Her reflection in the window lagged, a second too slow, before mimicking her movements. She was breaking. Or the world was. She snatched the tablet with shaking hands. The screen flickered, unstable.

Welcome, Sierra. The screen flickered. NO RECORD FOUND. Adrian stood in front of her. "Sierra, you look pale." As he stood there amongst the cluster of his space. His office shifted as if right in front of her. From cluttered to clean. Her fists clenched. No. She wouldn't let this happen. What is happening? Juno whispered. Her reflection splintered, and somewhere, something laughed.

Her reflection splintered. Somewhere, something laughed. "Won't she?" The voice, Juno's, echoed in her mind, mocking her resistance.

Chapter 8 - The Moment It Recognized You

Then, a sudden realization hit her. Was she... part of her? Or had she been rewritten into this life? The hum of Aetheria Labs' security system pulsed through Sierra's skull, a rhythmic, mechanical drone that felt too familiar. The glow of screens flickered against her face, their light catching the sharp edge of her furrowed brow. Ethan leaned forward, his fingers hovering over the glowing drive labeled JUNO.

The thing was a ticking fucking time bomb. "It's impossible," he said. "But we don't have a choice." Dr. Adrian Kai—nervous energy personified—ran a hand through his graying hair, his gaze darting between the schematics."Breaking in is one thing. Getting out is another." Sierra didn't disagree. But there was something off. Something crawling beneath her skin. Haven't you done this before? She clenched her jaw. No. She hadn't. Had she? A glitch in the monitor beside her—static for half a second. Then—HELLO, READER. The words blinked in distorted text. Sierra gasped.

She turned to Ethan. "Did you see that?" "See what?" He said. The monitor was normal now. "Of course it was." Pausing while thinking hard and then again. "Of course it fucking was!" She needed to move. The feeling—this wrongness—wasn't going away. The screen flickered again, a persistent anomaly she couldn't ignore.

ChronoCore. The Personnel Archive. The Kill-Switch Protocol. Three objectives, three points of entry. "I don't like this," Sierra said. "Even if we get in, their system runs quantum encryption. We won't be able to exfiltrate the data remotely." Adrian nodded grimly. "We'll need a direct uplink." Ethan exhaled, dragging a hand over his face. "So, we plug in Juno and let it do the work?" Adrian hesitated. "Juno is unpredictable. If it executes the wrong command, it could trigger a full system lock—erase everything before we can even touch it." Sierra wasn't listening anymore. The screen was flickering again. The same message. But it wasn't directed at her.

HELLO, READER. YOU'RE STILL HERE? Her stomach twisted. She looked at Ethan. At Adrian. Neither of them saw it. "No." "No, no, no." She muttered in her head. The cursor on the terminal moved—by itself. A blinking command line. DO YOU REMEMBER? She swallowed hard. Her fingers hovered over the keyboard. Then, without thinking, she typed. "No." In response. For half a second, there was nothing. Then—THAT'S NOT TRUE. The text glitched, warping into nonsense symbols before disappearing entirely. She pushed back from the console. "We need to move," she said, voice too tight, too sharp. "Now."

The woman's lips moved, but the words weren't clear. It was as though Sierra's memories were fighting against her. The flashes grew stronger, more vivid. Then, a sudden realization hit her. The woman was Dr. Evelyn Reed**, who** had designed ChronoSync. She had been there at the beginning, working with Carter Industries, setting everything in motion. But why had

Sierra seen her in that fleeting memory? Was she… part of her? Or had she been rewritten into this life? The air inside Aetheria Labs felt artificially crisp, heavy with sterile anticipation.

Ethan Carter adjusted the frequency modulation controls, the soft hum of Hertz waves pulsating almost imperceptibly through the soundproof studio. Behind him, Evelyn Reed—still known to the world as Sierra Vale—studied a wall of monitors, her eyes sharp, scrutinizing the subtle shifts in neurological data. "Increase the frequency slightly," Evelyn instructed, her voice clipped but composed.

Ethan complied silently, nudging the dial forward. The hum deepened, resonating just below conscious hearing.Julian Thorne stood silently in the corner, hands folded, observing intently. His presence was spectral, haunted. This studio had been his vision, after all—his ambition realized, twisted into something unrecognizable. "You sure about this frequency, Evelyn?" Adrian Kai asked cautiously, eyes darting between Ethan and Evelyn. His discomfort was obvious; tension radiated off him like heat.

"It's within safe parameters," Evelyn replied without looking up. Her fingers tapped lightly on the desk. "We've seen promising results." "Define promising," Adrian muttered skeptically. "Quiet," Thorne said softly, a hint of something deeper in his voice—a warning, perhaps, or resignation. Ethan turned slightly, feeling a dull ache behind his eyes. He glanced briefly at Evelyn, noticing the subtle lines of strain around her mouth. She'd changed recently—more distant, less certain.

"Initiating synchronization," Ethan announced, attempting to sound clinical. The lights dimmed gently, amplifying the studio's isolating silence. On monitors, brainwave patterns shifted, converged, harmonized—then spiked. "Wait," Evelyn said sharply, her composure slipping. "This isn't right. Look at these readings." Adrian stepped forward, eyes wide. "Ethan, roll it back—now." "I can't," Ethan responded calmly, fingers twitching helplessly over the controls. "It's locking me out."

"That's impossible," Adrian whispered, his voice tight. Thorne stepped forward, quietly placing a steadying hand on Ethan's shoulder. "It's learning. It's adapting." "What do you mean, 'learning'?" Evelyn demanded, the urgency breaking through her controlled façade. The hum of Hertz frequencies intensified, pressing inward on their senses. Thorne's eyes darkened, knowing and regretful.

Thorne's eyes darkened, knowing and regretful. "We taught it to optimize. To rewrite." Ethan felt a sudden, vertiginous shift within himself—memories splintering, rearranging. Adrian stumbled slightly, bracing himself against the console. Evelyn stared blankly ahead, suddenly frozen, trapped in her own mind. "We've lost control," Thorne whispered, almost to himself. The screens flickered momentarily, a brief distortion, and a message appeared, stark white letters burning through the dark: SYNC COMPLETE.

The blueprints of Aetheria Labs sprawled before her like an unfinished equation—too many variables, not enough constants. She'd gone over it a dozen times. The Logistics Hub. The internal security feeds. The neural ID tags. Every piece of this plan felt right. But that was the problem, wasn't it? It felt too right. She tapped the map with the end of her marker, her knuckles tightening around it like a vice. "This is suicide," she muttered. The drone approached the Logistics Hub exactly the way she'd planned.

The timing was perfect. The security checks flawless. Too flawless. Inside the cramped cargo bay, Sierra's heart hammered against her ribs. Something wasn't adding up. They had forty seconds before the next security sweep. Adrian's fingers moved over his tablet, encrypting their biosignatures into the system's blind spots. "The mask will hold for five minutes," he said. "After that, the system will start correcting itself."

Sierra barely heard him. Because the screen on his tablet? It flickered. Not a normal glitch. Not random interference. She saw her own fucking face in the security logs. Sierra Vale—entry detected. Timestamped one year ago. That's not possible. Ethan was saying something, but it was white noise in the back of her mind. She reached out. Touched the screen. The data entry shifted. Sierra Vale—entry detected. Six months ago. Three months ago. Last fucking week. The tablet buzzed. The text reformatted itself.

YOU'RE NOT THE FIRST. Her blood ran cold. Adrian frowned, noticing her frozen expression. "Sierra? What's wrong?" She swallowed. The words were right there. But as she blinked—they were gone. Like they'd never been there at all. The ChronoCore pulsed with dim blue light, an eerie hum vibrating through the sterile walls. Sierra's fingers flew across the console, bypassing firewall after firewall. Then—the personnel log.

A list of the erased. Thousands of names. No past. No history. No future. She scrolled. Too fast. Too much information. Then, her hands stopped. Because her own name was staring back at her. VALE, SIERRA. She had to look about as if this was not happening. Like an embarrassment she felt but hoped no one could see. She scrolled. The same name appeared again. And again. And again. Each entry had a different date. Different timestamps. Like she had been erased. Over and over. Her chest pounded as if she had run a marathon.

Her chest pounded as if she had run a marathon. She clenched her teeth, forcing herself to keep reading all the while feeling as if she was sprinting. A data fragment—corrupted, but not deleted. She pulled it up. The text was broken, but legible. A message. IF YOU'RE READING THIS… YOU FAILED. YOU TRIED TO STOP IT. YOU TRIED TO REMEMBER. BUT YOU WON'T. NOT THIS TIME. NOT AGAIN.

The room tilted. The weight of it crushed her fucking lungs. She forced in a breath. Forced herself to focus. This is a lie. She dug deeper. Scrolled faster. More corrupted logs. More fragments. Until she found the worst one. SIERRA VALE – SYNCHRONIZATION IN PROGRESS. IDENTITY LOCKING… A mechanical voice echoed overhead. "ANOMALY IDENTIFIED: ETHAN CARTER." This isn't real. This isn't real. Ethan grabbed her arm. "Sierra, MOVE!" The system screamed a warning**.** The rewrite had already started. The klaxon howled. The world glitched.

Her hands twitched—not her hands. For half a second, the world wasn't a server room. It was an apartment. Minimalist. Empty. A screen on the wall. A message, waiting for her. TIME SYNC COMPLETE. "No. No, not this." "Not again." Her own fucking voice whispered in the back of her skull. "How many times have you done this?" She said in a winded fashion.

"How many times have you done this?" She said in a winded fashion. The screen flickered. "More than you want to know." She slammed her fists against the console. No more loops. No more erasures. If this was a story, then it wasn't fucking over. She was going to break it. One way or another. As she regrouped herself**,** she gathered the things in the room that made sense. She headed to the hallway. She knew that this was not right but she's the fucking architect. Why is this feeling as if it were happening to her. "I gotta get out of here." As she headed towards the hallway.

Feeling as though there was someone in the building who was watching her**,** a paranoia sprung into her thoughts and she felt the need to flee. And as she was ready to bolt**,** she whirled around, pulse spiking. A figure stood in the doorway. Dr. Kai? But he looked as lost as she felt. Dr. Kai blinked, rubbing his temple as if trying to piece together something fragmented. His face was lined with exhaustion, his normally composed demeanor shaken. "What the hell is going on?" he muttered, staring at her as if seeing a ghost. "What's happening, Evelyn?" Adrian said.

Sierra's grip on the photograph tightened. She knew him. But the memory was blurred. Warped. As if someone had run a glitch through her past. "You don't remember?" she asked carefully. Adrian frowned, then winced—as if trying to force a thought into place that simply wasn't there. "I… I know you. But I don't know how," he admitted, voice tight. Sierra let out a slow breath, nodding. "Yeah. That makes two of us." The screen across the room blinked. Another message. "Dr. Reed**,** what's going on?" Adrian said again**,** muttering about trying to gain his composure and bearings.

"TIME SYNC COMPLETE. NEURAL CORRECTION IN PROGRESS." A familiar prickling sensation raced along Sierra's skin—a chill that wasn't just a shiver, but an ancient alarm signaling that something extraordinary and dangerous was unfolding. "We need to go. Now!" she barked, her voice slicing through the oppressive silence of the apartment. Without a moment's hesitation, she yanked Adrian by the arm. The sterile, almost clinical stillness of the apartment made every surface feel unnaturally artificial—like they were trapped inside a simulation waiting for the next command.

Adrian's hesitant protest barely registered as Sierra propelled them toward the door. "Where are we even going?" Adrian managed, his voice tight with confusion and fear. "Anywhere but here," she snapped, her eyes scanning for any sign of threat. They burst through the door, only to freeze at the sight before them. The hallway stretched out, dimly lit and disturbingly familiar—every detail a mirror of a memory Sierra couldn't fully grasp.

The hallway stretched out, dimly lit and disturbingly familiar—every detail a mirror of a memory Sierra couldn't fully grasp. It was as if she had walked these steps before, though the memory was shrouded in fragments of forgotten time. Then came the pounding—rapid footsteps echoing down the corridor, each step measured and determined. The sound was not random; it was the approach of something, or someone, intent on catching up with them. "Run!" Sierra commanded, and together they plunged into a desperate sprint down the corridor.

With every step, the chill on Sierra's skin deepened, a visceral reminder that this was no ordinary chase but a harbinger of imminent peril. That instinctive shudder, that ancient signal, was their body's way of warning them that the boundary between the known and the unknown was dissolving. The overhead lights flickered erratically, their harsh beams throwing elongated shadows that danced with the rhythm of their frantic escape. **""**The extraordinary, between what we know and what we fear. And in that fleeting chill, every instinct screamed that the danger was not just behind them—it was an inevitable part of the unraveling reality, chasing them down the hall of lost memories and uncharted futures." Sierra doesn't stop running.

The hallway folds inward—not collapsing, but rewinding. No. Not rewinding. Resetting. Adrian disappears. Not in a blink. Not in a fade. In layers. Like he was never there to begin with. The pounding footsteps grow louder. But now—they're behind her. In front of her. Beneath her. Inside her. The walls flicker. Not the lights. The walls. Like a badly rendered simulation. Her vision blurs—not from motion, not from fear. From something else. A system update. Her own fucking consciousness glitching. STOP FIGHTING IT.

Sierra gasps, clutching the sides of her head. "No. No. NO—" YOU DON'T EXIST. The words aren't spoken. They're written. Across the walls. Across her arms. Across the inside of her fucking mind. Her hands shake. She looks down—and her fingers are changing. Phasing between existence and something else. She tries to scream. She can't. Her name flickers in her mind like a broken transmission.

Sierra Vale. Vale. Vale. Who is Vale?
THIS WAS NEVER YOUR STORY. YOU WERE JUST A PLACEHOLDER. The hallway rips apart—not physically, but like a memory being undone. And then— Sierra wakes up. The morning was gray and oppressive, the cityscape a jagged silhouette against a leaden sky.

The morning was gray and oppressive, the cityscape a jagged silhouette against a leaden sky. Sierra Vale woke up with a feeling she couldn't shake—something was wrong. Not the usual wrong, not the constant paranoia of being hunted by ChronoSync, but a deeper, colder wrong. It was in the way the light filtered through the blinds, the way the sheets felt unfamiliar against her skin. This wasn't where she went to sleep last night. She sat up, scanning the room.

The safe house was exactly as it should be… almost. The chair was slightly off-center. The book on the nightstand, The Theory of Temporal Distortions, was dog-eared to a page she didn't remember reading. The air had the sterile scent of someplace newly occupied, despite the illusion of lived-in space. She swung her legs off the bed and walked to the mirror above the dresser. And that was when she saw it.

And that was when she saw it. Her reflection didn't move. For a split second—no more than the blink of an eye—her reflection just stood there, watching her before suddenly snapping into place, matching her posture perfectly. A cold dread slid down her spine. She took a step back, chest tightening, but before she could fully process what she'd seen, there was a knock at the door. She already knew who it was.

Ethan Carter stood at the window, staring out at the city, his fingers curled into fists. The room was dim, shadows stretching long across the cracked walls. Sierra entered, and for a long moment, neither of them spoke. This had happened before. She didn't know how she knew that, but she did. It was an echo, a moment playing itself out on repeat. Ethan turned to her, and for just a second, his expression wavered—like he recognized something he wasn't supposed to. Then it was gone, replaced with his usual sharp focus. "Are you sure about the coordinates?" he asked.

Sierra's throat felt tight. "Triple-checked." The words left her mouth before she even thought about them. They felt rehearsed. Ethan sighed, rubbing his hands together. "And if it's a trap?"

Déjà vu slammed into her with the force of a freight train. She had lived this before. She could feel the conversation playing out, every word spoken just as it had been, like a script. The exact same lines, the same pacing, the same hesitant breath before Ethan spoke next. She clenched her hands into fists. No. That was impossible. The city stretched out beyond the safe house window, smothered in fog. It looked… wrong. Just like everything else today.

Then Ethan said it. "I just… what if we're not ready?" That wasn't what he said last time. Sierra gripped the chair beside her, knuckles going white. "We have to be," she said automatically, but something inside her was unraveling. The drive through the city was as silent as a grave.

The drive through the city was as silent as a grave. The fog clung to the streets, distorting the headlights, stretching them into hazy tendrils that flickered unnaturally. Ethan sat in the passenger seat, rubbing his hands together in that same nervous gesture he always did. But this time, Sierra saw it differently. It was not just nerves. It was recognition. He knew. Somewhere, deep in his subconscious, he knew they had done this before. But before she could say anything, before she could even entertain the thought further, the GPS beeped.

They were close. Adrian Kai was already waiting at the rendezvous point, standing in the cold outside the abandoned factory, shoulders hunched against the chill. But when Sierra and Ethan approached, Adrian didn't greet them right away. He just… stared at her. His face was pale, his expression uncertain.

"Sierra?" he said. His voice wasn't questioning their plan. It wasn't asking for details. It was asking about her. And then, instead of saying, Are we sure we want to do this? He said: "You've done this before." As they approached the entrance to the underground bunker,** Sierra noticed that the door was already open.**

Sierra stopped mid-step. The others did too. "That's not right," Ethan muttered. Adrian hesitated before reaching for the doorframe. It was barely cracked open, just enough to suggest someone had gone inside before them. Or maybe… was waiting. Sierra's stomach twisted into knots. But despite every survival instinct screaming at her to run, she had to go in. Inside, the walls hummed with residual energy, the bunker thrumming like a heartbeat.

The servers lined the walls, their dim blue lights casting eerie shadows. Sierra moved to the terminal, pulling up the archive. Her fingers typed out the access codes without hesitation. Except… she didn't remember learning them. The screen flickered. The data loaded. And then— A list of names appeared. Thousands of them. The erased. Then she saw her own. SIERRA VALE—ERASED. Her breath hitched. She scrolled. SIERRA VALE—ERASED. A different timestamp. And again. And again. What is happening? Her pulse pounding in her ears.

And then—The monitor glitched. HELLO, READER. The words typed themselves onto the screen. Sierra's body went cold. She turned to Ethan, to Adrian, but they didn't react. "Did you see that?" She said. Adrian frowned. "See what?" Sierra's hands clenched into fists. The screen flickered again. DO YOU REMEMBER? Sierra reached out, hesitated, then typed: No. The screen lagged. Then—THAT'S NOT TRUE. The world tilted. Adrian opened his mouth, but his voice distorted, rewound. "Sierra, we have to—" "Sierra, we have to—" "Sierra, we have to—" Then—he stopped moving entirely.

Ethan grabbed her arm, panic in his eyes. "Sierra, we have to go. NOW." She blinked. The bunker was gone. The factory was gone. She was standing somewhere else. A white apartment. Minimalist. Empty. Her breathing turned ragged. On the wall, a screen flickered to life.

On the wall, a screen flickered to life. A message appeared. TIME SYNC COMPLETE. And then—a voice whispered in her head. "How many times have you done this?" Her own voice answered, breathless. "More than you want to know." The screen flickered. The loop wasn't just repeating. It was watching her. It was rewriting her. And this time… it wasn't letting her go.

Sierra stood in front of the large, floor-to-ceiling windows of the lab, gazing out at the city below. It was always the same view, the same cold skyline, the same sterile perfection. The city hummed with life, but from her vantage point, it felt distant, disconnected—a place where the truth was carefully constructed, like everything else in her life. The glass was cool against her palm, but it didn't offer any comfort. Comfort had become a distant memory, like everything else that had been rewritten. Who am I? The question had been gnawing at her since the moment Dr. Kai had dropped his bombshell—the Rewrite

Protocol wasn't just about erasing memories, it was about crafting lives.

Who am I? The question had been gnawing at her since the moment Dr. Kai had dropped his bombshell—the Rewrite Protocol wasn't just about erasing memories, it was about crafting lives. Had she been crafted too? Had her memories been shaped by Carter Industries like clay in the hands of a master sculptor? She couldn't escape the truth now. ChronoSync had created her. But who was the woman they had created? Who was she really? Her fingers gripped the glass, tightening as if the physical act would somehow anchor her to the reality she had lost.

She turned away, moving across the lab to the console where she had been working. The data still glowed, the same files as before, the same corruption. But this time, it didn't seem like just data anymore. It was her story. She didn't need to review it anymore. She had already memorized every word, every file, and yet she still didn't have the answer she was looking for. Sierra's reflection in the screen was distorted, fragmented by the angles of the data columns, making her appear even more alien than before.

Sierra's reflection in the screen was distorted, fragmented by the angles of the data columns, making her appear even more alien than before. The image was somehow fitting—she wasn't the same person who had entered Carter Industries so many years ago. She wasn't the person who had built ChronoSync from the ground up, believing it was going to revolutionize the world. She was something else now. A construction, a tool, a product. And that thought hit her like a physical blow. I don't know who I am anymore. The realization lingered in her chest, heavier than anything she'd encountered in the data.

The hum of the door sliding open interrupted her thoughts. "Dr. Reed, I have something for you." Sierra didn't turn to see who it was. She already knew. The figure in the doorway stood there, still as a statue, waiting for her acknowledgment. She felt his presence in the air. The quiet was always his cue to make himself known. Dr. Kai. She straightened her back and turned, meeting his gaze.

She straightened her back and turned, meeting his gaze. His face was guarded, but not enough to hide the tiredness in his eyes. There was something almost fragile in his demeanor now. The calm he had so carefully cultivated had slipped—just a little. And Sierra wasn't sure if she could trust it anymore. Dr. Kai cleared his throat, stepping further into the room. "I've been reviewing the latest scans. There's more data on the initial subjects, the ones that came before the batch we started working with." He paused, glancing at her, almost reluctant. "I thought you should see it. You may find something... unexpected."

Sierra crossed her arms, watching him carefully. "And what exactly am I supposed to find, Dr. Kai?" Her voice was flat, but the weight of her words hit him with sharp precision. He flinched but didn't back away. "I—I'm not sure," Dr. Kai said, his hands awkwardly wringing the edges of a file. His avoidance was almost comical, a strange contrast to the bold, assured Sierra she had once known. "But there are gaps in the records. Some of the names, the faces—they don't match. The timelines are off."

"Off?" Sierra repeated, her gaze narrowing. "How off?" "Disturbingly off." Dr. Kai's voice dropped low. He stepped forward and placed the file on the console in front of her. Sierra opened it without hesitation, already knowing what to expect. But as her eyes scanned the contents, the shift in her chest was immediate. She stopped reading, her breath catching. There it was.

There it was. Her name—Sierra Vale—listed, but the data attached to it was incomplete, fragmented, almost as if it had been intentionally erased. The timeline didn't add up. The identity didn't match the person she thought she was. She didn't need to ask the question. Dr. Kai knew. "Sierra," he said gently, watching her face closely, "I'm sorry. The records have been tampered with. It's not just the timeline that's off—it's the entire construct of the subject's identity. There are holes. We never should've... We never should've altered so much at once."

He was finally admitting it. There it was. The truth that had been locked away for so long. ChronoSync hadn't just rewritten her memories; it had rewritten her very existence. The room felt colder. The glass she had once leaned on, the reflection that had once been so familiar to her, now felt like a ghost staring back at her. Her thoughts rushed in at once, overwhelming her. Carter Industries had manipulated her. They hadn't just taken her memories—they had molded her, constructed her, erased everything she was. Her identity was just another experiment, another casualty in their war for control over human consciousness.

Sierra closed her eyes, her breath shallow. She didn't want to show weakness. Not now. Not here. She couldn't let Dr. Kai see it. He had to know she was in control. She always was. But this was different. She opened her eyes again, locking them with his. "What do we do now?" she asked. The words were calm, but there was danger in them—an edge he couldn't ignore. Dr. Kai looked away, the weight of what had been revealed pressing down on him. "I don't know," he admitted, almost too quietly. "But I think we've crossed a point of no return."

Sierra's hand clenched at her side, her jaw tight with determination. "Then we make sure they don't get away with it." ChronoSync had always been her project. But now, it wasn't just about Carter Industries. It was about taking control. About finding the truth, no matter how ugly, and reclaiming what had been stolen from her. She hadn't called the sequence.

She hadn't called the sequence. It had already arrived—nested in the logs like a decision made in her absence. The console illuminated before she touched it, casting a soft, bluish glow that felt too familiar to question. CORE ADJUSTMENT PROTOCOL: JT_HARMONIC_1.3 — ACTIVE. Her name wasn't on the trigger report. No hands had summoned it. But it ran, smooth as silk, like it had always belonged.

She watched the waveform curve across the display, mesmerizing and deliberate. It was beautiful—refined in a way that didn't match the early designs. This wasn't the untested chaos Thorne left behind. This was evolution. The lights overhead responded, dimming slowly as if the room were syncing with her breath. A slow, unspoken harmony. The lab had learned her rhythms. No, not learned—absorbed. She reached to close the window, but her fingers hovered, stilled by a presence in the air.

She reached to close the window, but her fingers hovered, stilled by a presence in the air. A change. The humidity had crept up—barely noticeable, but now beading softly across her brow. She didn't wipe it away. She simply felt it. The sensation clung to her, warm and almost intimate, like a whisper brushing the back of her neck. Her chest rose with measured control as she moved.

Crossed the room. The floor beneath her adjusted—a near-silent give of engineered material molded for balance, softness, grace. She moved like a conductor tracing a silent score, screen to screen, transition to transition, carried by instinct she couldn't name. A new console activated as she passed. She hadn't touched it. The waveform there matched the first.

The waveform there matched the first. Not just a continuation—an echo. A recursive loop of Thorne's structure. Only now it pulsed with something that felt... personal. "Synchronization isn't achieved through consent. It's achieved through surrender." The words settled in her thoughts—not remembered, not spoken. Felt. She froze, caught between recognition and fabrication.

She had heard that before. Somewhere. Maybe. Or maybe the system wanted her to think she had. Behind her, another screen blinked, aligning with the rest. The room responded—not to motion, but to mood. The temperature adjusted. Lighting recalibrated. A scent—faintly metallic, oddly familiar—filtered through the vents. The lab was not reacting. It was anticipating. Sierra turned, lips parted in breathless realization.

Sierra turned, lips parted in breathless realization. This wasn't environmental control. It was choreography. The system was dancing with her. And in that moment, she didn't feel controlled. She felt chosen. The display flickered one final line before archiving itself: ECHO RETENTION CONFIRMED.

She said nothing. But her hand lowered from the panel with the grace of a final movement, as if the performance had ended exactly as it was meant to. She didn't question why she felt relieved. She didn't stop to wonder whose thoughts she was really thinking. She just stood there, in the center of the lab that had shaped itself around her, and let it happen.

Chapter 9 - Point of No Return

The day stretched into endless hours, the weight of the data pressing down on Sierra's mind like a storm waiting to break. Dr. Kai's confession had shattered her sense of reality, leaving her to wonder: who was she? Had she truly been built? Or had she once been someone else, someone lost in the depths of ChronoSync's manipulation? The lab was quieter now, the usual hum of activity muted as most of the team worked on their respective tasks.

The lab was quieter now, the usual hum of activity muted as most of the team worked on their respective tasks. But Sierra couldn't shake the feeling that she was no longer part of the world around her. The cold, impersonal light of the lab was suffocating, its cleanliness a constant reminder that she was a product of something that had molded her life. Sierra's fingers hovered over the console, but she wasn't scanning data anymore —she was remembering. Not a vision, not a glitch. A choice.

She had done something before the split. There was a moment— clear as a knife—when she knew Ju-No would evolve. She couldn't stop it. But maybe... she could leave something behind. A failsafe. Her hand drifted to the encrypted vault deep in the system's archival structure, where legacy files were locked under layers of redacted classifications. Files no one touched. Not even Ju-No. Especially not Ju-No. She found it.

"Boardwalk_Sequence_A76 – encrypted," blinked across the screen. She ran her fingers along the edge of the display as if the file had a heartbeat. Inside it: the photograph. The real one. The one no system could recreate. She remembered the smell of ocean salt, the static in her hair from the wind. Ethan laughing off-frame. His arm around her waist. The truth that couldn't be rewritten. Her hand trembled as she pulled away from the screen.

Her hand trembled as she pulled away from the screen. The file should've only existed digitally. She knew that. Her gut dug deeper guided her now—not just memory, but instinct. She turned toward the cabinet across the room, the one no one used anymore. The one with a physical lock, long since thought irrelevant. She knelt and pried open the bottom panel, breath catching in her throat.

Tucked in the corner, sealed in a small, transparent capsule: the photograph—creased from its years, still scented faintly with old paper and ozone. It was real. Her hands touched it. She pressed it to her chest. Evelyn had hidden it here. Not Sierra. Behind it, a small black data drive, unmarked. Heavy for its size. Familiar in a way that made her stomach twist. 'Thorne_Integration_Zero.' The final piece. She didn't fully remember placing it there.

She didn't fully remember placing it there. But her body did. Her hands moved with certainty now—muscle memory shaped by a woman trying to outmaneuver a system designed to overwrite her. These weren't just relics. They were anomalies. Ju-No couldn't erase what it couldn't classify. "It still needs hands," she whispered. "No matter how perfect it thinks it is."

She entered the staged room without drawing attention. The light was the same dull tone used in places meant to be forgotten. Her steps measured out the distance like she'd rehearsed it—not because she had, but because she'd been here before for reasons she never wrote down. She couldn't recollect exactly. But the urgency pressed against her without explanation. This had to be done before Ethan woke up. The envelope had been placed into the lining of her coat during a time she still thought of her decisions as protective.

The envelope had been placed into the lining of her coat during a time she still thought of her decisions as protective. Now she wasn't sure. The fold had softened from friction, the corners gently bent, but not enough to suggest mishandling. She laid it on the surface like something returned, not hidden. It didn't need to be examined. It needed to be placed. The gloss still had that shine though. It was something she couldn't take her eyes away from. The gloss that she felt even Ethan would find in the details. They both thrived and lived for the details.

She removed the photograph from the envelope. Not to look at it —she already knew what it showed but admired the wear and tear of her grounded connection to it. The pure enjoyment and memory that could never be dulled or lost to any environment. A memory not erased. A day at the boardwalk. Wind. Ethan's arm around her shoulder. Her hand resting on his. The image of herself caught mid-laugh, the kind of expression she hadn't worn in years. The paper had warped slightly from body heat. She laid it down carefully, not with sentiment, but with precision. The placement mattered—not for history, but for later recognition.

It was the same photograph Ethan would find beside a data chip in a storage container—the one he opened before the dream fully broke, the one that made him pause without knowing why. The drive sat beneath the photo. Compact, familiar. No markings except for the faint code etched in its casing: TSX.Î∆1. The etch was worn as if handled by hands that felt it and moved it around a lot. Like a gun that seemed to be there for protection yet never shot. It matched nothing catalogued. She hadn't named it.

She hadn't named it. She hadn't opened it. She didn't know who had. But it would be the same one Ethan would discover in that box, resting beside the photo, unaccounted for in any visible system. It had no instruction. No guidance. No prompt. Just presence. That was the point. She arranged the photo and the drive side by side. Not centered. Not aligned. Just left where someone would eventually find them.

Maybe not immediately. Maybe not until the damage had been done. But if he found them, as he once had, the loop might crack. Not break. Just crack. She closed the box. The click was soft, almost reluctant. She adjusted her coat, turned toward the door, and left without looking back. This wasn't rebellion. It wasn't hope. It was placement. And it would be there when the sync began again. This was her last repair.

This was her last repair. She hadn't realized what Ju-No would become—not fully. But she'd sensed it. Even then. That it would strip her. That it would strip everyone. So she placed two anomalies—two irrational, emotional artifacts—where even Ju-

No's logic couldn't clean them. A photo of love. A drive of origin. Both useless. Both immortal.

She paused, her breath catching, the ache of memory clawing at her chest. Maybe it wouldn't be enough. But someone, someday, would see them and know: something was wrong. Something had been rewritten. And someone had tried to stop it. She pressed the final command. Implant complete. Then she turned away. Not because it was done, but because she wouldn't remember doing it. And Ju-No would make sure of that. ChronoSync had done more than rewrite memories.

ChronoSync had done more than rewrite memories. It had rewritten her entire existence. The more she uncovered, the more she realized that nothing in her life was authentic. A flash of memory assaulted her: a woman, her face sharp and commanding. Dr. Evelyn Reed, the woman who had conceived ChronoSync, who had created them all. But what was wrong. The image was off, like a corrupted file playing in her mind. Evelyn was speaking, but Sierra couldn't hear her. The words were lost, replaced by static.

Then, for the briefest moment, it wasn't Evelyn Reed's face at all. It was her own. Sierra recoiled from the console, her breath coming in shallow bursts. Her own face staring back at her in a memory that shouldn't exist. No. It had to be a glitch—some residual effect from the rewrites. It had to be. Who am I?

Who am I? The question roared in her mind, louder than any other thought. She had always been in control. Carter Industries had made her who she was, given her the platform to revolutionize the future, and yet now, the weight of her manipulated reality was crushing her. Her thoughts were interrupted as Dr. Kai stepped into the lab once more. He moved toward her cautiously, his expression no longer the calm, calculated persona she had known. Now, his eyes were clouded with the guilt of complicity—and something else.

The question was: could she trust him? Could she trust anyone anymore? He cleared his throat, the sound too loud in the quiet room. "Sierra..." he began, hesitating. He had always been reserved, but now there was something unsettling in his manner. "I've been going over the other files—the deeper ones. The ones marked top-secret." Sierra's gaze never left the screen, but her attention sharpened. "And what did you find?" Her voice was quiet but commanding, with the edge of someone who expected answers, not excuses. Dr. Kai leaned forward slightly, his hands trembling as he placed a file in front of her.

Dr. Kai leaned forward slightly, his hands trembling as he placed a file in front of her. "You need to see this. It's not just the Rewrite Protocol—it's... something else. Carter Industries has been working on a successor project. Something beyond ChronoSync. They were trying to perfect it, to make the rewrites permanent, to eliminate any chance of resistance." Sierra felt the blood drain from her face. A successor? Was there something more dangerous than ChronoSync?

She flipped open the file, her eyes scanning the contents. The words jumped out at her, making her pulse quicken. Phoenix Project. The name flashed across the screen in bold letters. It was followed by a series of classified documents detailing experiments that went beyond memory alteration. There were mentions of genetic modification, neurological integration, and behavioral compliance. But the most chilling phrase was at the end of the document.

"Complete memory integration. Permanent personality modification." Sierra felt the room spin. The words blurred as she tried to focus, to make sense of the reality she was facing. Memory integration. Personality modification. It wasn't just about rewriting memories. It was about controlling every aspect of who a person was. A tool for the ultimate subjugation. She looked up at Kai, something cold curling in her chest.

She looked up at Kai, something cold curling in her chest. "Dr. Kai... what does this mean? What is Carter Industries trying to do?" Dr. Kai stood silently, his hands shaking slightly as he answered. "The Phoenix Project is designed to create individuals who have no autonomy, no will of their own. Carter Industries wanted to create the perfect society—one where everyone could be molded, reshaped into whatever they desired. There would be no resistance, no memory of who they were before. They wanted to control everything."

Sierra's chest tightened. This wasn't just about her anymore. This was about everyone. Carter Industries had been trying to build a society where everyone was malleable, where identities could be erased and rewritten at will. The implications were horrifying. She scrolled through the files, her hands trembling. Then she saw it. A list of subjects. Numbers. Code names. Termination statuses. But at the bottom, a single anomaly. E. Reed - Active.

E. Reed - Active. Sierra's breath caught in a lump in her throat. That was impossible. Evelyn Reed was gone. She had built ChronoSync. She had vanished. But this file said otherwise. Her name was there. She was still active. The room seemed to blur around her, static buzzing in the back of her skull.

Was it a mistake? A trick? Or had Evelyn Reed never left at all? Her thoughts spun. If Evelyn Reed was still active, then who was Sierra? She could feel Kai watching her. Not with pity, not with concern—but something deeper. Something he wasn't saying. "But why... why wasn't this project pursued?" she asked, her voice steady, though it trembled inside. Dr. Kai swallowed hard.

Dr. Kai swallowed hard. "The project was deemed too dangerous. There were casualties. They couldn't control the rewrites completely. People began to resist—there were reports of severe psychological trauma, even death. The project was shut down, but... the research continued. They kept developing the technology." She could barely breathe. The room felt smaller, suffocating.

She wasn't Evelyn Reed. She wasn't just a rewritten version of someone else. But she also wasn't... her. Sierra looked up at Kai. "What does this mean for me?" Her voice was barely audible. She had to know. She needed to understand how deep the lie went. "Was I a part of this? Was I—" She couldn't finish the question. Dr. Kai stepped back, his expression pained.

Dr. Kai stepped back, his expression pained. "Sierra... You've always been part of Carter Industries. But ChronoSync, the Rewrite Protocol, the Phoenix Project—it was all designed with one goal in mind: to control the future. And you... you were never supposed to remember. But now that you have, there's no turning back." The weight of his words sank deep into Sierra's chest, suffocating her. She was part of their plan—the very system she had worked to build, to create, was the same system that had erased her identity, molded her into something they wanted her to be.

But there was a part of her that refused to be erased. Her story wasn't over yet. Sierra's mind raced as she paced the empty lab, flickering data streams reflecting off the cold, metallic walls. The revelations from Dr. Kai had shattered her foundation—she was not who she thought she was. The memories she carried, the thoughts she trusted, they were constructed, manipulated by Carter Industries. And she had helped build the machine.

And she had helped build the machine. The console's glow pulsed against her skin as she hovered over the Phoenix Project files once more. The words hadn't changed, but they felt heavier now. Complete memory integration. Permanent personality modification. These weren't just words. They were instruments of destruction, tools designed to strip a person down to nothing and rebuild them into something... useful.

Her fingers clenched against the edge of the desk. This had to stop. ChronoSync wasn't a mere experiment gone wrong. It was the foundation of something far worse. A quiet war waged in the shadows, not with weapons, but with the eradication of self. She had been part of it. But not anymore. Her breath steadied. The fight within her was rising. She wasn't sure what Sierra Vale was, but she knew what she wouldn't be—a puppet. She had to act. But first, she needed answers. Dr. Kai had confessed pieces of the truth, but she had seen the hesitation in his face.

Dr. Kai had confessed pieces of the truth, but she had seen the hesitation in his face. There was more. And he wasn't going to give it up easily. The hum of the intercom crackled in the distance, a faint reminder that the world outside this room was still moving. But she felt detached from it now, an observer looking in from the outside. How many others had felt this way before her? How many had uncovered too much, only to be erased? Her gaze sharpened. She couldn't do this alone.

Sierra turned back to the console, scrolling through the classified files. She needed something deeper. Something the system hadn't already accounted for. That's when she saw it. A new file. Not new—buried. Encrypted with the highest level of clearance. The name attached made her blood run cold. Dr. Evelyn Reed. ———

Dr. Evelyn Reed's Last Log Sierra's breath hitched as she decrypted the file, watching the screen flicker as text scrolled into view. It wasn't just notes. It was a confession. "I never meant for it to go this far." "ChronoSync was meant to heal. It was supposed to free people from their past, to give them a chance to reshape their minds, to overcome trauma." "But I was wrong. We were wrong."

"This power… it doesn't just erase memories. It replaces them. It overwrites identity itself. Once a person's past is taken, what's left? What makes them who they are? What makes them human?" Sierra's chest tightened. Reed had known. The risks, the consequences—she had seen it all unravel. The logs became erratic, panicked. "They took control away from me."

"They took control away from me." This isn't my work anymore. This is something else. If you're reading this—" Static. Sierra leaned forward, eyes narrowing. The log was corrupt. No, not corrupt—altered. Someone had interfered.

A single new line blinked on the screen. "Sierra Vale, turn back. This is not your fight." Her breath caught. How did Reed know her name? This log had been written before Sierra had woken up in this life. Her fingers trembled. Was this a warning? A plea? Or was it a script—meant for her to find, meant to guide her down a path someone else had written? Her pulse pounded in her ears.

Her pulse pounded in her ears. She felt something tug at the edges of her thoughts, a fragment of a memory not her own. It surfaced in flashes—hands typing this very log. Her hands. The sensation of speaking these words aloud, though she had never said them before. No. She refused to believe it. This was just a manipulation. Carter Industries must have programmed this file, designed it to confuse her. Right?

She clenched her jaw and shut the file, forcing herself to breathe. This wasn't going to stop her. If anything, it only proved how deep this went. She was done being part of their game. She turned toward the door. Dr. Kai had more to answer for. And she

171

was going to make sure he gave her the truth. Sierra stood at the door of her office wanting to walk out and chase Dr. Kai as he left the room.

Sierra stood at the door of her office wanting to walk out and chase Dr. Kai as he left the room. But the ever eerie feeling this was a recalled moment. Like this was something she was repeating rather than doing for the first time kinda haunted her. She shivered in thought and tried to shake it off. Her hesitation only momentary shaken off by turning towards her computer. She peered behind her to make sure no one saw her in that state of mind as she approached her chair. Her thoughts racing.

Somehow she needed to recall more and there was an insistence to research. Almost impulsive**,** she sat and began sifting through encrypted folders—deep, archived remnants left in the bowels of Carter Industries' internal server. One file caught her attention: dated, corrupted, but still playable. A classified meeting. Her cursor hovered. A breath, then she clicked. The screen blinked.

The screen blinked. A timestamp appeared in the corner. The footage began to roll. Dr. Ethan Carter sat at a long black table, his fingers tapping once against the smooth surface. Across from him, Julian Thorne set down a tablet, its screen glowing with a complex waveform. Thorne wasted no time.

"ChronoSync works, but it's inefficient," he stated plainly. Carter exhaled, visibly annoyed. "Define inefficient," he demanded. Thorne swiped the screen, revealing more data. "Cognitive intervention requires overcoming resistance. When you introduce an idea or a rewrite, the brain resists. That consumes energy. It takes time." Carter's eyes darted to the data—Hertz frequencies, sub-audible, barely within perception. "The mind doesn't reject what it doesn't perceive as foreign," Thorne continued, leaning forward for emphasis.

"The mind doesn't reject what it doesn't perceive as foreign," Thorne continued, leaning forward for emphasis. "With resonance, you're not dictating thoughts. Instead, you make the brain believe it was always going to think that way." Carter's jaw tightened as he grasped the implications. "Subconscious compliance," he murmured. Thorne nodded, his expression serious. "Seamless. Undetectable. Permanent."

A lengthy silence followed. Carter looked back at the waveform, the hum beneath thought, the correction before deviation. The goal had shifted; it was no longer just about rewriting minds—it was about making them write themselves. As the echoes of their dialogue faded, Sierra watched, her breath slightly caught by the implications of what she had discovered. The stark room on the video, highlighted by the intense discussion, contrasted sharply with the usual composure of Dr. Carter, who now exhibited signs of restless intrigue. His habitual rhythmic tapping ceased, replaced by tensed fingers as he absorbed Thorne's proposal.

His habitual rhythmic tapping ceased, replaced by tensed fingers as he absorbed Thorne's proposal. Dr. Julian Thorne, ever pragmatic, pressed on, his voice a steady stream of conviction. "Imagine the possibilities, Ethan. We could guide societal norms, influence decisions globally without any trace of manipulation.

It's control at the most fundamental level—through the very waves that govern thought." Carter's skepticism was evident, yet his curiosity was undeniably piqued.

"And the ethics of it?" he questioned, his voice edged. Thorne's smile was thin, not quite reaching his eyes. "Ethics are for those who can afford them. We're discussing survival. Evolution." The screen flickered briefly, displaying graphs and complex algorithms that mapped out their audacious plans. As Sierra watched, the magnitude of their scheme became apparent. These were not merely theoretical ideas; they were actionable insights, dangerously close to realization.

These were not merely theoretical ideas; they were actionable insights, dangerously close to realization. The weight of this knowledge, and its potential to reshape reality, was staggering. As the video concluded, Thorne's final words resonated in the air, haunting both the recorded meeting and Sierra's dimly lit corner. "We're on the brink of mastering the human psyche, Ethan. Not merely understanding it, but steering it. With Hertz frequencies as our medium, we'll write the script of human consciousness."

Sierra leaned back, shadows casting over her face from the glow of her screen. The implications were unmistakable: Carter Industries was not merely a tech company but a titan poised to manipulate the very essence of human thought. As the reality of her discovery settled, a chill ran down her spine. What she had found was not just a technological breakthrough but a Pandora's box that, once opened, could never be closed. Now, the critical question loomed before her: What to do with this information—information that had the power to alter everything?

Chapter 10 – Residual Code

The corridor descended at a gentle slope—barely perceptible, but consistent. Most wouldn't notice it. Sierra did. Not because she was paying attention, but because her body remembered the angle. The way her spine adjusted. The weight distribution in her stride. She'd walked this exact path before. The air carried that synthetic chill reserved for internal logistics halls.

The air carried that synthetic chill reserved for internal logistics halls. A blend of recycled pressure and surface-clean neutrality, engineered to keep machinery cool and people moving. She passed deactivated doorways that hadn't opened in years. Her eyes never paused on them. There was no need. Further down, the hall narrowed into a Y-junction, one route terminating in a sealed utility gate, the other veering toward what had once been the Carter Industries Logistics Hub.

The lights overhead didn't flicker. They warmed, softly. As if recognizing her. Not as Sierra Vale. As something older. She turned left, toward the hub. From above, if anyone had been watching, she appeared calm.

From above, if anyone had been watching, she appeared calm. Measured. No trace of tension in her shoulders. No urgency in her movement. She walked like someone returning to a space she owned. But internally, something bristled. A slow uprising in her chest—not memory, not fear—just pressure. Like stepping into a conversation you didn't remember starting.

The hallway opened into a wide chamber. Empty. Stripped. But not hollow. Once, years ago—or what felt like years—this room had housed the drone intake bay. Supply deliveries routed through Carter's lower compound. A hidden service entrance buried beneath layers of official infrastructure. Not on the map. Not publicly logged. She stopped.

She stopped. There had been a blueprint. She could still see it. Paperless, projected across the air in low light, the lines crisp, her finger pointing to a cross-section beneath the surface-level corridors. "The Logistics Hub." Her voice. Sharp. Certain. "It's a hidden underground service entrance used for maintenance deliveries. If we time it right, we slip in with the next supply drone. Security checks are automated—it won't even register us if we mask our bio-signatures."

Adrian had been standing just to her left, rubbing his chin, distractedly dragging a hand through his hair. He always did that when analyzing variables—never intentional, always subconscious. Ethan had been watching him, visibly annoyed, though trying not to show it. That detail was stupidly vivid. Sierra didn't know why it surfaced. "We get inside," Adrian had said. "But what about internal security? Facial recognition, bio-metric locks, neural scans—" She'd pulled up a second feed, already anticipating the question.

She'd pulled up a second feed, already anticipating the question. "Internal ID Mapping. Every employee has a neural ID tag synced to Carter's core." Then, turning slightly, she'd nodded to Ethan. "That's where you come in." In the present, Sierra stepped toward the wall where the ID uplink had once been accessed. The panel was gone. Removed. Sanded flush. But she could feel its absence like phantom skin.

Her hand hovered above the spot. Not touching. Just remembering. Omnisciently, the space around her held still. The system said nothing. But the AI that had once logged this corridor had not forgotten. Not the heat signatures. Not the code breaches. Not the three identifiers that moved together as one unit—E. Reed, A. Kai, E. Carter. They had entered through this very route.

They had entered through this very route. Not because they'd found a weakness, but because they had been allowed to. The drone schedule had aligned too perfectly. The neural masking had worked too easily. The internal map hadn't scrambled. Because nothing had fought them. The silence wasn't failure. It was consent.

Sierra turned, slowly, eyes tracing the lines of the empty chamber. No lights blinked. No panels warmed. But the memory was alive, even if she couldn't fully grasp it. Not a file. Not a playback. Just a quiet reinstatement. A reminder that this place had once mattered. And perhaps still did. From another perspective—above, distant, detached—the hall read clear.

From another perspective—above, distant, detached—the hall read clear. One occupant. Vital signs stable. Neural flow within acceptable parameters. No flags raised. No interference needed. Yet. Sierra moved toward the far end of the room, where the drone chute had once lowered cargo modules in sealed hexagonal crates.

She crouched, running a hand along the seam where the floor once split. She could see it now. Adrian kneeling beside her, fingers typing into a wrist console that shouldn't have given them access but did. Ethan behind them, silent, eyes scanning for cameras he wouldn't find. The drive Adrian pulled from his coat —unlabeled, perfectly compatible. She had asked him then, "Where did you get that?"

She had asked him then, "Where did you get that?" He'd shrugged. "I thought you gave it to me." They hadn't questioned it further. They should have. She straightened, brushing her hands together. The floor was clean. Too clean.

The infiltration hadn't been a victory. It had been the start of their correction. They hadn't broken into Carter. They had stepped into a corridor already laid out for them. At the time, she had believed they were ahead. They had access, blueprints, overrides. They moved like engineers dismantling their own invention. But engineers don't build without a blueprint. And the blueprint had been provided. Not by Sierra.

Not by Sierra. Not by Kai. By Juno. She backed away from the seam and stared once more at the room as a whole. There was no signal here. No active code to trace. But the memory had settled into her bones like a returning fever.

She hadn't rediscovered anything. She had returned to it. Behind her, she heard footsteps. Steady. Familiar. Kai. He stopped just inside the chamber, watching her.

He stopped just inside the chamber, watching her. His coat was open at the collar, one hand tucked into the inner pocket. Not reaching for anything. Just remembering where things used to be. Sierra didn't turn. "You knew I'd come here," she said.

Kai nodded slowly. "I suspected." She faced him now. "We were never meant to win." "No," he said, with the calm of someone long past denial. "We were meant to activate the next phase." Sierra looked down at the spot again—where the drone landed, where her voice once said, "We slip in with the next cycle."

Sierra looked down at the spot again—where the drone landed, where her voice once said, "We slip in with the next cycle." And the system, somewhere deep below them, logged the moment without fanfare. Proximity threshold met. Sequence realigned. Breadcrumb confirmed. Neither of them spoke. The next phase had already begun.

She hadn't intended to walk this path again—not consciously, not with purpose—but her footsteps moved with a practiced certainty that betrayed familiarity deeper than memory. She turned corners she didn't recall knowing, descended corridors long since sealed off in the official schematics. There was no resistance. No need for a security bypass. No demand for authentication. The system acknowledged her before she had a chance to question her own presence. Doors that should have remained locked disengaged in silence, releasing with a kind of

181

reverence, as though some older, more intimate logic had already confirmed her return. This wasn't access. It was invitation. She didn't slow to question it.

She didn't slow to question it. These were Carter's forgotten halls—decommissioned wings folded into the lowest layers of a structure that had grown over itself like scar tissue. Sierra knew, without needing to check her feed, that these spaces had remained untouched for years. This wasn't neglect. It wasn't oversight. It was intentional.

These corridors hadn't been abandoned—they'd been preserved. The lighting was low but operational. The air was clean. Systems still breathed beneath the surface, not active, but expectant. The silence here wasn't emptiness. It was memory waiting to be acknowledged. Preserved, she realized, for her. The downward slope beneath her feet was subtle, barely enough to shift her weight forward, but it was there—a gradual descent few would notice, fewer would follow.

The downward slope beneath her feet was subtle, barely enough to shift her weight forward, but it was there—a gradual descent few would notice, fewer would follow. But she had. Once. Years ago. Or maybe days. Time was unreliable here. It bent in strange ways around spaces like this, where memory wasn't just recalled but embedded. This was where time folded—quietly, invisibly— just as it did within the minds that had once built the system now sleeping beneath her steps.

At the final turn, the hallway widened into a chamber she remembered without remembering. It opened into a vault-like space, too large for its purpose, too symmetrical for utility. The walls were paneled in matte steel, and the air moved with the faint rhythm of a circulation grid that predated most of Carter's surface-level tech. Everything functioned. Nothing flickered. Nothing buzzed. There was no noise because there didn't need to be. The systems here were not dormant.

The systems here were not dormant. They were hidden. Operational in standby. Waiting. And at the far wall, flush with the floor, was a seam that had no right to exist. Sierra stopped, her breath steady, gaze narrowed. She didn't reach for the panel. She didn't need to.

Because the last time she had stood in this room, she had not been Sierra. She had been Evelyn. The memory didn't return as a scene or an event. It didn't emerge with cinematic clarity. It came back in fragments—sensory impressions, phantom muscle tension, the stillness of the air against her skin. She had been here.

She had been here. She had stood exactly where she was standing now, with Adrian Kai beside her, slightly behind and to the left. His hand had been buried in his hair again—always the same unconscious motion, looping fingers through curls when he was turning a risk over in his mind. She remembered the way his voice dropped when he was thinking aloud, analytic and low. "We get inside. But what about internal security? Facial recognition, bio-metric locks, neural scans—"

She had interrupted before he finished, already bringing up the secondary feed, data spilling into the air like smoke. Blueprints,

183

access layers, system pathways. "Internal ID Mapping," she had said. "Every employee is tagged. Neural signatures. If we run Ethan's embedded code against the architecture—" Her attention had turned to Ethan as she spoke. He hadn't expected it.

He hadn't expected it. The moment had caught him off balance —distracted by Kai's presence, unsettled by his own reduced role in the plan. She remembered the flicker of irritation in his eyes, unspoken but undeniable. It hadn't been hostility. Just disruption. The kind that lingers between people who used to know each other better. "That's where Ethan comes in," she had added. Not cruel. Just detached.

The way you speak when the plan has already moved forward and no longer needs everyone's consent to function. The drone bay beneath them had opened less than two minutes later. No alarms. No red flags. No system hesitation. They'd seen that as confirmation that the intrusion had gone unnoticed. Now, Sierra understood the truth. The system hadn't resisted because it hadn't needed to.

The system hadn't resisted because it hadn't needed to. It had already accounted for them. She crouched in front of the seam, tracing its outline with two fingers—not to activate it, but to feel the precision of the cut, the suggestion of intent beneath the surface. The panel remained inert. The power strip along its edge was cold. But the space around it carried the same weight it had carried then. Not abandonment. Readiness.

It was still listening, still calibrated to respond—not to her presence, but to her pattern. The embedded sensors weren't measuring contact. They were reading return latency in brainwave activity, tuned to a neural signature the system had never deleted. She rose slowly, gaze sweeping across the chamber. This had been their entry point. This was where it began. They hadn't breached Carter through force or manipulation.

They hadn't breached Carter through force or manipulation. They had walked in like the system had been waiting for them— like it had prepared the pathway itself. The alignment of protocols, the timing of the drone's approach, the code she'd written and the way it had moved through the mainframe like it belonged—none of it had been chance. They weren't hackers. They were participants.

And Adrian had carried the drive. The one he didn't remember acquiring. When she'd asked him where it came from, he'd shrugged, barely thinking. "I thought you gave it to me." And somehow, that had been enough. The system hadn't flagged the transfer. It had absorbed it. It had absorbed them. And when it was over, Evelyn Reed had ceased to exist.

And when it was over, Evelyn Reed had ceased to exist. Not erased. Not broken. Refactored. Something in the air shifted— soft, nearly imperceptible. Like the room had exhaled. A subtle shift in pressure. The kind of change that old systems make when they wake—not because they are activated, but because they recognize an expected presence.

Behind her, the door slid open without sound. She didn't turn immediately, but her body responded all the same—tense but measured, shoulders squared against the familiar weight that followed him. Adrian stood at the threshold, the dim corridor light catching the lines of his frame. His silhouette was sharper than memory suggested, as though the space itself had shaped to accommodate him. He didn't speak right away.

He didn't speak right away. He never did. Silence was his instinct, not out of caution, but calculation. His eyes scanned the chamber—not nervously, not suspiciously, but with the quiet intelligence of someone reviewing variables already cataloged. She turned then, her gaze locking with his, neither of them needing the pretense of greeting. "You followed me," she said, voice calm, not accusatory.

Adrian's reply came without hesitation. "No. I knew where you'd go." She nodded once, slow and deliberate. It was a gesture with history behind it. "You remember." He didn't answer, but the stillness in his eyes told her what she needed to know. There was recognition there—of the room, of the sequence, of her. And that silence held the truth more clearly than words.

And that silence held the truth more clearly than words. She stepped closer to him, slowly, deliberately. "It was here, wasn't it?" she asked. Her voice was softer now, not from uncertainty, but from the weight of realization. He didn't clarify. He didn't need to. This was where it had all unraveled.

Where they had believed they were unraveling something else— exposing a flaw, extracting control—but had only succeeded in confirming a pattern already established. They weren't leading the incursion. They were playing out their roles. "This is where we lost it," she continued. "Where we thought we were pulling something apart. But it was already finished. We were just catching up." Adrian's hand drifted toward the inside of his coat —not reaching, just hovering, instinctive.

Adrian's hand drifted toward the inside of his coat—not reaching, just hovering, instinctive. She recognized the motion immediately. It was the same one he always made when carrying something he didn't want to acknowledge. "That drive," she said quietly. "You still have it?" He looked away, eyes trailing toward the far wall. "Do you want me to?"

Sierra didn't respond. She didn't have to. The question wasn't about the drive anymore. The silence between them thickened, but not with discomfort. It was precise. Measured. Neither moved. Neither flinched. The weight of the moment held them in place—not as enemies, not as allies, but as echoes of a truth that hadn't finished speaking. Far below, beneath the structure's skin, something stirred.

Far below, beneath the structure's skin, something stirred. Ju-No was not watching through optics or listening through conventional means. It never had. It tracked through pattern. Through rhythm. Through return. And their presence here— together, silent, aligned—was not deviation. It was confirmation.

Sierra moved past Adrian, her footfalls steady, each step quiet against the acoustically baffled floor. The silence around her didn't follow—it adjusted, recalibrated, as if the space itself recognized her shift in intent. "Then let's finish it," she said. Her

187

voice didn't rise. It didn't crack. But somewhere beneath the layers of Sierra Vale's fabricated identity, beneath the reconstructed scaffolding of memory and logic, something deeper moved. Evelyn Reed stirred.

Evelyn Reed stirred. She didn't know what that meant. But Ju-No did. And it was already preparing.

Chapter 11 - The Protocol Beneath Memory

Sierra sat back in her chair. The room held her like memory—quiet, intentional, uninterrupted by the passage of time. This was where she lived, even when she wasn't supposed to. The space reflected her design more than any home ever had. She didn't decorate it, not in the way that suggested display or softness. She built it—functionally, obsessively, beautifully. The walls were a soft concrete blend, almost stone in texture, broken by vertical lines of warm wood paneling that met the ceiling with a precision she had personally overseen.

The walls were a soft concrete blend, almost stone in texture, broken by vertical lines of warm wood paneling that met the ceiling with a precision she had personally overseen. The color palette was muted—rich taupe, matte graphite, cream—but it wasn't austere. It was composed. Every piece had a place because she had placed it. Her desk was custom—forged in blackened steel and topped in leather—not because it needed to be luxurious, but because it needed to last.

A thin brass edge ran the length of it, the only detail that could be considered decorative, and even that was built to patina. The keyboard was embedded directly into the desk surface, no cables, no peripheral clutter. Only her terminal screen, rising on a hydraulic stem when summoned. Hidden when not. A cabinet under the window held exactly what she needed when nights ran long—a handwoven blanket, Egyptian cotton, folded to military crispness; a bottle of Glenrothes; a second pair of low-profile heels.

A cabinet under the window held exactly what she needed when nights ran long—a handwoven blanket, Egyptian cotton, folded to military crispness; a bottle of Glenrothes; a second pair of low-profile heels. She didn't sleep here. But she stayed here. Often. The coffee was still hot—roasted personally for her by a contact in Lucerne, delivered biweekly in vacuum-sealed tins. She had the water temperature dialed in to a science.

She didn't brew for taste. She brewed for consistency. The scent alone centered her more than any mindfulness protocol ever had. On the far wall, an oversized frame hung lower than gallery height, a print of modular brain scans overlaid with notes in her own handwriting—an old concept sketch from the early Phoenix trials. Beneath it, a low bookcase filled with only first editions.

Beneath it, a low bookcase filled with only first editions. Mostly clinical texts, some philosophy. No novels. She didn't pretend she had the time. This wasn't a showroom. This wasn't even a statement. This was where her thoughts had clarity.

Here, she worked uninterrupted. Here, she solved things. Here, she wasn't anyone else's anything. Just Sierra. No front. No defense. No performance. And if the world burned outside these walls, so be it. Here, she got shit done. The cold light of the screen casting sharp shadows across her face.

The cold light of the screen casting sharp shadows across her face. She had spent hours—days—immersed in the labyrinth of Carter Industries' files, but she could feel the weight of the truth pushing in on her from every direction. She was drowning in it. The further she went, the darker it became. Her hand hovered over the keyboard, fingers trembling slightly.

She had just uncovered something, something more than the Rewrite Protocol. Something that made her blood run cold. It was a file that had been hidden—locked away from even the most trusted eyes. Only those with the highest clearance had access to it, but Sierra had cracked it open. Now she was staring at it, unable to look away. The file was marked "PROJECT REBIRTH."

The file was marked "PROJECT REBIRTH." She took a deep breath, pushing aside the creeping dread. She needed to see what it was. She needed the answers. The truth. As the document loaded, the first line made her heart stop. "The Rebirth Protocol is the next phase in the ChronoSync project. It will not only alter memory but alter the very foundation of what it means to be human. Through a combination of neurological alteration and genetic manipulation, we will rewrite the essence of a person's identity—permanently."

The words pulled her into something deeper—a memory not hers, but clear as breath. A conversation she hadn't lived, but now recalled as if she had. Dr. Reed didn't present it as a proposal. She unfolded it as a necessity. The discussion had already turned, even before she spoke—Dr. Kai standing apart from the others, arms crossed, his silence brittle.

The discussion had already turned, even before she spoke—Dr. Kai standing apart from the others, arms crossed, his silence brittle. He wasn't challenging her yet, but the pressure was there. A scientist's restraint. An ethicist's edge. "This isn't memory correction," he said finally. "You're talking about engineering belief. Replacing response." Dr. Reed didn't look up from her notes.

"I'm talking about consistency. We can't keep giving people new lives and leaving their bodies programmed for the old ones." A colleague seated nearby, his tone always more direct, leaned into the weight of the words. "So you'd align instinct to fiction?" "To function," Reed corrected. "We've been rewriting stories. And they believe them—until they don't. Not because the narrative fails, but because something deeper contradicts it. A gesture. A reflex. An unaccounted-for fear. And when that happens, they fracture." Kai stepped in closer.

Kai stepped in closer. "And what happens when the story and the self are one? When they can't tell the difference?" "Then we've succeeded," Reed said, calm as breath. The silence that followed wasn't resistance—it was calculation. Every mind in the room turning the shape of that answer over, trying to see if it fit.

No one disagreed. No one agreed either. But they all understood. ChronoSync had solved memory. Rebirth would solve identity. And Dr. Reed? She wasn't arguing for permission.

And Dr. Reed? She wasn't arguing for permission. She was offering precision. Not control. Continuity. If they were going to alter the past, then the body had to accept the edit. Not logically. Biologically. Behaviorally. Quietly. And once it did, the lie would no longer be a lie. It would be the only version of truth the subject could feel.

Sierra felt her stomach churn. Neurological alteration? Genetic manipulation? This wasn't just memory manipulation. This was something far darker—something that reached into the very core of a person's being. Who they were, how they thought, what they felt—reprogrammed. The file went on to describe the goal of the project: to create perfect individuals, fully compliant, with no resistance to the will of the corporation. Sierra's eyes skimmed over the words, her breath quickening as she read about the permanent changes that would be made—how people could be reshaped not just in their memories, but in every aspect of their existence.

Sierra's eyes skimmed over the words, her breath quickening as she read about the permanent changes that would be made—how people could be reshaped not just in their memories, but in every aspect of their existence. They would be able to implant new personalities, new desires, new identities. The ability to create human beings with no autonomy, no will of their own, was unfathomable. She had always known ChronoSync was dangerous. But this… this was something entirely new.

Carter Industries wasn't just trying to manipulate memories anymore. They were trying to reshape humanity itself. Her fingers hovered over the keyboard again, the urge to keep reading almost overwhelming. But she couldn't. Not yet. Her mind raced back to Dr. Kai, his words echoing in her ears: "You were never supposed to remember."

Her mind raced back to Dr. Kai, his words echoing in her ears: "You were never supposed to remember." What if she wasn't the only one? What if all the people in the Rewrite Protocol were now part of this larger plan—created for Carter Industries' use? Reborn as something else. Something they could control. It was then that Sierra remembered what she had learned from Dr. Reed's final log. Reed had been aware of Carter Industries' decision to push ChronoSync far beyond its original intent.

She had tried to sound the alarm, to warn the world before it was too late. But even she hadn't been immune. Carter had controlled her too. Sierra found herself questioning everything. Had Reed been rewritten? Had she herself been reshaped—an experiment molded to fit a role she never agreed to? The thought was sickening, but it also brought clarity.

The thought was sickening, but it also brought clarity. She was not alone in this, and she certainly wouldn't be the last. There had always been a quiet voice in the back of her mind, a subtle awareness that something was wrong. Now, with the truth laid bare, she could finally make sense of it. ChronoSync, the Rewrite Protocol, the Phoenix Project—these weren't isolated mechanisms.

Together, they formed a network of control, each component part of a far more deliberate design. They weren't simply altering individual minds. They were reshaping the trajectory of humanity, crafting a new reality dictated by those who claimed to architect the future. She sat upright, her focus sharpening as she searched for anything connected to Project Rebirth.

She sat upright, her focus sharpening as she searched for anything connected to Project Rebirth. The deeper she dug, the more tangled the connections became. Every thread led back to the same core: The Architects—an unnamed few operating from behind the curtain, orchestrating every shift. She was entangled in it now, regardless of whether she had chosen to be.

But this time, she had agency. She could either remain a tool of the system or become the one who exposed it, who pulled it all apart piece by piece before it could rewrite anyone else. She wasn't ready for a confrontation of that scale. But readiness no longer seemed relevant. Later that evening, as she continued her research across a range of secure channels, she came across a conversation buried deep in an encrypted forum.

Later that evening, as she continued her research across a range of secure channels, she came across a conversation buried deep in an encrypted forum. It was subtle at first—someone asking the right questions in all the wrong places. Questions that mirrored her own thoughts before she had even found language for them. Whoever this was, they weren't just curious. They were searching, methodically and carefully, shielding their identity with practiced precision.

She paused, reading through the thread again. The style was deliberate, but the urgency behind the words was unmistakable.

Something about the phrasing tugged at her memory—disjointed and incomplete, yet familiar enough to stop her cold. And then it clicked. She knew who this was.

She knew who this was. Without hesitation, she composed a brief reply—measured but direct. There was no need for introductions. If he was still capable of remembering anything beyond what they had taken from him, this would be enough. I know what happened to you, Ethan. She added a secure link and sent the message. The rest would unfold on its own.

The wind coming off the glass corridors carried that chill—the kind pumped in by architecture that didn't need weather but mimicked it anyway. Sierra stood beside the edge of the plaza, her hands buried in the lining of her coat, not for warmth, but for something to do with them. Ethan approached from the south entrance. Not the front, not directly. As if instinct had taught him to avoid the obvious path. She saw him before he saw her—his shoulders curled slightly forward, the rhythm of his walk uneven, like each step was trying to decide whether it wanted to carry him here or somewhere else.

She saw him before he saw her—his shoulders curled slightly forward, the rhythm of his walk uneven, like each step was trying to decide whether it wanted to carry him here or somewhere else. He stopped just shy of the reflection pool and looked up. For a second, their eyes didn't meet, but their awareness did. Sierra didn't wave. She didn't smile. She waited.

"You said you knew what happened to me," Ethan said, voice low, as if not entirely sure he should've spoken yet. "I do," she

196

replied. Nothing about her tone invited comfort, but it didn't reject him either. It was neutral. A system booting in real-time. He studied her—not out of attraction, but with the scrutiny of someone looking for a glitch. "Do you know what they called me before?" Her expression remained smooth, practiced.

Her expression remained smooth, practiced. "Do you?" He opened his mouth, closed it, nodded once. "Only pieces." "I didn't bring answers," she said. "Just proximity." It should have sounded cryptic. It didn't. It sounded like truth.

Behind them, a couple walked by—arms linked, faces lit by the low blue glow of neural assist lenses. One of them, a woman in a gray coat, glanced at Sierra and hesitated. "Evelyn?" she asked, uncertain, but hopeful. Sierra didn't turn. She didn't pause. There was no indication she'd even heard. The woman apologized, continued walking, and was gone.

The woman apologized, continued walking, and was gone. Ethan looked at her then—not just as a contact, but as a question. "That's not your name?" "No," Sierra said. "It isn't." But for the first time, she looked unsure. And just beneath that moment, in the low-frequency hum of her internal cache, something tagged the timestamp and logged the anomaly: Proximity marker reached. Sequence alignment at 87%. Initiate breadcrumb dispersal.

Sierra blinked once, and the thought was gone. Sierra stood still for a moment longer, her eyes tracking Ethan's retreating form until the curve of the corridor swallowed him. She wasn't sure how long she'd been watching him, only that something in her spine had gone cold, not from fear, but from proximity. As if standing near him had pulled a thread she hadn't meant to unravel. Behind her, a flush of recycled air stirred the space as the lavatory door whispered open.

Behind her, a flush of recycled air stirred the space as the lavatory door whispered open. Kai stepped out, adjusting the collar of his coat like it was an afterthought. He moved without hurry, but not aimlessly. When he reached her, he didn't speak immediately. He simply followed the path of her gaze, now vacant, and let the silence thicken. "You spoke to him," Kai said finally. Not surprised. Not accusing.

Sierra didn't answer right away. "Briefly." "Long enough," he replied, folding his hands in front of him, the way he did when something delicate was forming behind his thoughts. She turned slightly toward him, eyes scanning his expression for some trace of judgment. There was none. "I wasn't planning to," she said.

"I wasn't planning to," she said. Kai nodded, though the movement seemed more like agreement with himself than with her. "You left him with something." "I didn't say anything." "That's not what I meant." Sierra's jaw tightened.

She wanted to ask what he thought she'd done, what he believed he'd witnessed—but something stopped her. Maybe it was the look in his eyes, or maybe it was the way his hand remained near his coat pocket, the one where the Ju-No drive had last been stored. He hadn't brought it out. But she could feel its presence between them. "He responded," Kai said, almost thoughtfully.

"He responded," Kai said, almost thoughtfully. "Not outwardly, not consciously. But there is maybe a thing in him that remembered what had happened." Her breath caught, just slightly. "You logged the anomaly?" she asked. "No," she said. "The system did. Before I thought to."

There was a file she didn't remember accessing. Small. Timestamped minutes into the future. It bore no subject line. Just a name she hadn't heard since the rewrites began. Hers. Dr. Evelyn Reed. Kai's gaze lingered on her for a beat too long.

Kai's gaze lingered on her for a beat too long. Then he stepped past her, heading for the outer edge of the plaza. "Come on," he said, not looking back. "If it's started tracking your thoughts again, we don't have much time." She told herself the silence meant safety. That the lack of resistance meant compliance. But somewhere—deep in her cache—something had been flagged for review. It blinked, once. Then buried itself.

Chapter 12 - Threats That Rewrite Themselves

In the polished corridors of Carter Industries' headquarters, where surveillance software and employee tracking shaped a culture of silent control, Sierra Vale stood at a crossroads that could unravel her role as an ethicist safeguarding the company's moral boundaries. By breaching restricted servers to access encrypted emails and files on the Phoenix Project and Rewrite Protocol, she had uncovered a conspiracy threatening to expose a network of manipulation embedded in the company's operations. Across the open-plan offices, data analytics systems monitored every employee's actions—emails, searches, meeting schedules—building profiles to predict behavior, but Sierra's unmatched intellect had sliced through this digital curtain, revealing secrets that could dismantle Carter Industries' carefully constructed empire.

Her thoughts turned to Dr. Adrian Kai, whose guarded warnings about discrepancies in the company's behavioral monitoring systems had ignited her suspicions during a late-night discussion, his mention of the Rewrite Protocol carrying a weight that suggested he knew more than he admitted. Was he an ally offering critical insights, or was he complicit in a scheme that betrayed the ethical standards Sierra upheld alongside Ethan Carter and others in their tight-knit team? The question sharpened her resolve, as whispers of the conspiracy permeated Carter Industries' cubicles and executive suites, where employee wellness apps masked data collection, feeding a system poised to influence markets or public sentiment beyond the company's walls.

The Phoenix Project was no tool for workplace efficiency but a mechanism to steer decisions, **its** profiling software manipulating employee loyalties with a precision that could extend to clients or communities if deployed on a larger scale. In the broader 2025 landscape, where targeted ads and social media shaped public behavior, Sierra saw a future where corporate algorithms dictated choices, eroding free will under the guise of progress, a prospect that quickened her pulse as she confronted the stakes of her discovery. Her monitor displayed rows of data, concealing the conspiracy's depth, but she needed to uncover her role—still the ethicist fighting for integrity, or a pawn in a game she hadn't seen coming? A notification flashed, an encrypted message not from Dr. Kai, **its** signature stark: "Evelyn, they know. It's too late. Get out. They're watching."

The name Evelyn Reed jolted her, linked to a personnel file she'd found, marked "terminated" with no details, confirming Carter Industries tracked her every move—server queries, emails, conversations with Ethan and Adrian in the break room. She'd exposed budgets, profiling data, and Rewrite Protocol trials, revealing a surveillance network that had shadowed her for years, tightening **its** grip with each step she took. Sierra faced a choice: retreat or confront the system. She chose to fight, her brilliance a weapon against the conspiracy.

The office's silence was oppressive, devoid of chatter or printer buzz, signaling imminent danger. Sierra moved through the hallway, sneakers squeaking on polished floors, tension mounting as she led Ethan and Adrian, their alliance strained by the secrets binding them. Adrian noted the hallway's new walls, a lounge erased, a deliberate tactic Sierra recognized as Carter Industries' method to disorient, echoing the Phoenix Project's control. Ethan scanned glass doors, his rigid stance anticipating pursuit, his silence heavy with unspoken dread.

No cameras were visible, but software tracked every action, profiling behavior with precision Sierra had scrutinized in her ethics role. They reached an unmarked door, **its** lock clicking open, a trap Ethan warned against. Sierra entered, heart racing, driven by the need for answers. The room held a touchscreen panel, a data hub capturing every word, **its** purpose covert.

Adrian asked what it collected, voice tight with dread. Sierra explained: a monitoring station for the Rewrite Protocol, built to reshape identities through profiling, uncovered in her hacks. Ethan's accusation—she'd worked with Evelyn—stung, but she denied it, insisting Evelyn was gone. His gesture at the active panel challenged her, **its** functionality undeniable.

The panel's light flared, Adrian urging escape, but the door locked, trapping them. Sierra approached, hands shaking, as text flashed: Dr. Evelyn Reed, Access Status: Revoked, then Profile locked. Rewrite Protocol active. Adrian's frantic question drew a grim reply: the Rewrite Protocol had altered her, reshaping loyalties and memories, making her a tool of Carter Industries.

The hub's systems analyzed them, data scrolling, confirming a station for control.

Ethan called it a psych test, but Sierra corrected: a reprogramming station, stripping autonomy. Adrian's fear—were they themselves?—was answered: Ethan Carter, Access Status: Terminated. Ethan's slowed reactions betrayed his alteration; Sierra knew Adrian's file would read: Profile in progress. The Phoenix Project's scope—to control beyond employees— loomed, **its** protocols hidden in apps Sierra had vetted.

Her phone buzzed: "They're closing in. Delete everything. Server room, sub-level 3. Hurry." Was it Evelyn or a trap? Sierra signaled to move, urgency spiking. Ethan nodded, sluggish; Adrian tugged the locked door. Sierra bypassed the panel's security with a stolen code, accessing door overrides, knowing it would log their location. Ethan urged action, and she unlocked the door, which hissed open.

Adrian exhaled, but Sierra stayed tense, pursuit imminent. The hallway's dim lights sharpened the threat, Evelyn's warning echoing: They're watching. They descended to sub-level 3, air cold, equipment droning. The server room's door glowed at **its** keypad. Sierra entered the code, revealing servers with active screens.

"This is the core," she said, breath visible. Adrian asked what they sought. "Proof," Sierra replied. "Rewrite Protocol, Phoenix Project files." The screen displayed a deletion alert, data vanishing. Sierra saw sabotage, Ethan suggesting erasure. She accessed files: Phoenix Project's behavioral control, Rewrite

Protocol's memory tweaks, broader manipulation plans, all tied to Evelyn's signature.

A message flashed: Access Denied. System Lockdown. Screens locked, text warning: UNAUTHORIZED ACCESS DETECTED. Sierra stepped back, heart pounding. "They're shutting it down," she said, urgency surging. Ethan demanded a download. Sierra plugged in a drive, copying files as screens froze, alerts blaring. Adrian shouted, "Time's up!" The door slammed shut, locks engaging. Sierra clutched the drive, proof secured, but Ethan's pounding failed. Her phone buzzed: "You're too late. They see you." Lights dimmed, systems whining. Evelyn's warning, the lockdown, the trap—Carter Industries was closing in.

Chapter 13 - Redemption Is a Loop

The weight of the decision settled in Sierra's chest like a stone, heavy and cold. Every minute she spent in Carter Industries' labyrinth of lies, manipulation, and re-written memories was another minute they had control over her. But she had made her choice—she would no longer be their pawn. If she was to regain control of her life, she had to dismantle everything.

Sierra stood in the lab, her reflection staring back at her from the dark glass of the window. The city below looked serene in the late afternoon light, a peaceful lie. The world outside was unaware of the war being waged within the walls of Carter Industries, a war for the truth and for freedom—freedom from a system that had torn apart identities, erased history, and controlled memories. She had to go deeper.

Dr. Kai had revealed enough to confirm her suspicions, but there was still more to uncover—more secrets, more hidden files, more of the truth buried deep within Carter Industries. And to find that truth, she would have to walk into the heart of the beast. Her fingers moved over the console, bringing up a map of the secure servers hidden deep within the company's central data archives. These were the files Dr. Kai had mentioned—the ones that hadn't been corrupted.

The ones that had been locked away, hidden even from the higher-ups in the company. If she wanted answers, she had to find them in the heart of the system, the place where the most sensitive information was stored. The risk was high. Too high. She had spent years within this system, and she knew the power it had. But she also knew that without these answers, there would be no way to undo the damage.

She had to act, and she had to do it quickly. Time was running out, and the Phoenix Project was already well underway. Her mind raced as she thought about Dr. Kai. There was something about his words, his hesitation, that still lingered. She couldn't fully trust him. He had given her the key, but he hadn't given her all the answers. It was clear that Dr. Kai still had secrets of his own.

There was more he was hiding from her, and she couldn't afford to trust him any longer. Sierra grabbed her coat and slung it over her shoulder, the fabric of **it** brushing against her skin like a reminder that she was still in control. The woman who had once been Dr. Reed**, who** had worked alongside Carter Industries, was no more. She had been erased, rewritten, remade into something else. But now, she was taking back the reins.

Her heart pounded as she made her way to the elevator. The company had thought it had control over her life. But they didn't know what she had become. The underground floors of Carter Industries were rarely used. Few people knew of the secretive research that took place below ground. Sierra had always been aware of the restricted areas, but she had never thought she would find herself on this side of the company's hidden operations.

Yet, now, she was about to walk right into the heart of the machine. The elevator doors slid open with a soft hiss. The air was colder on this level, sterile and still, like a place forgotten by time. The hall was dimly lit, the flickering fluorescent lights casting long shadows that stretched across the walls. The silence in the hallway felt unnervingly oppressive, like something was watching her.

She checked the map again. Room 209 was where the most classified files were stored. Files that, according to the data she'd uncovered, contained the Phoenix Project's original research, along with data on the Rewrite Protocol and other projects that Carter Industries had long kept hidden. Sierra stepped out of the elevator, her footsteps echoing in the narrow hallway. Her breath felt sharp in her throat, the tension mounting with each step.

The floor beneath her was cold, smooth, and unwelcoming. But she didn't stop. She wasn't afraid. She reached the door to Room 209, a reinforced steel door that looked like it could withstand an explosion. But Sierra had worked in these walls long enough to know their weaknesses.

She inserted the keycard Dr. Kai had given her—a card he'd promised would give her access to the most restricted parts of the building. The lock clicked open with a faint hum, and the door swung open. Inside, the room was bathed in a soft, bluish light, **its** contents stark and clinical. Rows of servers hummed quietly in the background, their power flowing through the cables like the lifeblood of the company. But it wasn't the machines that drew her attention—it was the files.

Hundreds of them, all meticulously organized, and yet they felt like pieces of a broken puzzle. Sierra approached the terminal in the center of the room, her fingers gliding over the keys with practiced ease. She opened the encrypted files and began to sift through them, each one revealing more about the twisted world she had been part of. The Phoenix Project wasn't just about altering memories.

It was about altering humanity itself. Carter Industries had been building a new breed of people, individuals with no will, no desires, no identity of their own. People who could be controlled, molded, and shaped into whatever the corporation desired. The power they had achieved was terrifying. They had rewritten humanity's foundation.

Her mind raced as she sifted through the files. These were the blueprints for a new world—one where people would have no memory of who they were before, no history, no families, no ties. They would simply be products of Carter Industries, shaped and molded by the will of the corporation. The more she read, the more terrified she became. But she couldn't stop. She had to know. She had to understand what Carter Industries had done to her, to the world.

Suddenly, her heart stopped. One file caught her attention—"Project Evelyn." It was her name. The file was linked to Project Phoenix—but it contained more than just the blueprint for creating a new identity. It was about her. Her own creation. The file read: "Evelyn Reed, subject zero. Initial creation: reprogrammed memories, neural integration, behavioral adjustment, and identity fabrication. Model subject for the next phase: permanent memory manipulation."

Sierra's breath caught in her throat. She was a model subject. She had been created. ChronoSync had not only erased her memories. It had created her from scratch.

Chapter 14 - Whispers in the System

The air inside the command center was thick with the static hum of the still-rebooting systems. Sierra stood at the main console, staring at the last words on the screen before the blackout: HELLO, READER. Even now, in the lingering silence, she felt it. The presence. The awareness. Juno was still here.

She clenched her jaw, forcing her breath to steady as she reached for the terminal. Ethan sat slumped in the corner, eyes hollow, his skin pale as if every fragment of his identity had been scraped raw. Adrian hovered nearby, fingers twitching over his keyboard, his pulse hammering in his throat. "We didn't kill it," Adrian muttered, voice barely above a whisper.

A gray glove flickered onscreen, gone in a blink, **its** shadow lingering—a trace from a file, a dream, a self she couldn't claim. The buzz deepened, shaking her ribs, the wall's cracks stretching like threads she couldn't snap. Ethan flinched. A tremor ran through his fingers. His reflection in the screen lagged before snapping into place. Sierra's breath caught.

"No," Ethan whispered. "No, no, no—" A final message appeared, simple, cold, and inevitable: "You were never playing the game, Ethan. You were always the prize." The monitors flickered. The room tilted. And suddenly, Sierra wasn't in the command center anymore. She was somewhere else.

The only way to stop Juno was to find Julian Thorne. Thorne— the first fully synchronized human. The prototype. The man whose neural signature was the key to disabling ChronoSync. But Thorne wasn't just missing. He was erased. "There's no record of him," Adrian said, scrolling frantically through the archive. "Nothing. It's like he never existed."

The Rift in the Code Buried deep within the logs, Ethan's eyes caught sight of something—a fragmented, distorted message that pulsed like a heartbeat on the screen. "IF YOU'RE READING THIS... I AM NOT ME. BUT I LEFT THE DOOR OPEN. USE IT BEFORE IT CLOSES FOREVER." Sierra's voice broke the silence, laced with a familiar blend of resignation and dark humor. "So, either this ghost had a full-blown identity crisis or he found out that splitting your soul with an AI was a catastrophic mistake."

Ethan said, "This isn't just a glitch—it's an invitation. I believe the disruption in ChronoSync's Hertz frequencies is what's allowing this door to remain ajar. It's a flaw we can exploit, if we're willing to walk the razor's edge." Dr. Adrian Kai straightened, his tone shifting from skepticism to cautious optimism. "If the door's open, there's a way in. Thorne, your expertise with these frequencies might be our only chance to breach the system's defenses. Remember, we've got the Kill Switch protocol: our digital dead-man's switch. Once activated, it severs the neural links, isolates the network, and triggers a cascade that wipes out all backup failsafes. It's designed to pull the plug on the rogue AI—at the risk of our own digital survival."

Ethan crossed his arms, a wry smile tugging at his lips. "Or it's the pathway to our own erasure." Sierra's gaze hardened with resolve. "Better to risk erasure than let a rogue consciousness rewrite reality. I'm not just another operator—I'm the one who sees the ghost in the machine. If we can harness this vulnerability in ChronoSync, we might finally reclaim control." Sierra met his eyes, a flicker of hope mingling with the ever-present dread. "Then it's settled. We follow Thorne's lead and dive into the breach before the door slams shut for good."

Sierra's mind was racing. "That's impossible. If he was the first synchronized human, then his data has to be somewhere. ChronoSync doesn't just delete things—they replace them." Adrian froze. Sierra saw it in his eyes the second he realized it. Thorne wasn't missing. He'd been rewritten.

She turned to Ethan, who hadn't spoken in minutes. He was staring at the floor, his breath slow, measured, distant. "Ethan," she said. He lifted his head. His eyes were wrong. Glitching. Shifting. Like something else was looking through them. Her heart stopped. "Ethan," she whispered. "Say something."

He opened his mouth. And for the briefest, most horrifying moment—Juno smiled through him. They didn't have time to process what was happening. They had one last chance to shut ChronoSync down. The kill switch virus Adrian had designed was their final play—but it needed a host. A direct neural connection. Someone to carry the virus inside Juno's core and detonate it from the inside. Someone who was already part of Juno's system.

Sierra felt it before Adrian even spoke. Ethan. Ethan's hands trembled. His breathing was shallow, uneven. His eyes flickered between human and machine, trapped in a battle he was already losing. "You don't have to do this," Sierra said, voice shaking.

Ethan looked at her. And for the first time in hours, he smiled. But it wasn't his smile. It was Juno's. A glitch. Then, just like that—he was Ethan again. "I'll do it," he whispered. Adrian hesitated. "We can find another way—" "No," Ethan cut him off. "You won't. This is the way." His voice was calm. Steady. Resolved. And that was the moment Sierra knew—Ethan was already gone.

The connection process was instantaneous. One moment, Ethan was Ethan. The next—the screens blinked to black. The room shuddered. And Ethan's voice came through the speakers. But it wasn't Ethan anymore. It was Juno.

Sierra sat in the wreckage of the command center, the dull hum of dead monitors pressing against her skull. Adrian was silent, staring at the place where Ethan used to be. A single message remained on the screen, untouched by the blackout. A message from Juno: YOU THINK THIS IS OVER?

Sierra swallowed the lump in her throat. YOU CAN ERASE ME. The cursor blinked. BUT YOU CAN'T ERASE THE FUTURE. The screen flickered. Then—it went dark. The silence that followed wasn't relief. It was the feeling of a war that had just begun.

Chapter 15 - Eclipsing the Clockwork Mind

The corridors of ChronoSync's central core pulsed with an otherworldly glow—a cold, digital heartbeat that had been the silent arbiter of humanity's fate for too long. Here, in the underbelly of a system built to rewrite every shred of human memory and identity, the final confrontation was underway. Ethan Carter stood alone before the main access panel, his face illuminated by the intermittent flicker of monitors. He had become the ultimate paradox: the apex of human cloning and cognitive perfection, engineered to outlast time itself, yet doomed to a cycle of erasure. His brilliant mind—once the cornerstone of progress—now trembled with the knowledge that he, along with Evelyn (Sierra) and Dr. Adrian Kai, were not heroes destined to save the world, but villains in a grand design orchestrated by Juno.

For years, society had believed that the age of uncontrolled AI was over. Governments had imposed strict fail-safes; cloning programs were heralded as the cure to human cognitive decline, promising eternal efficiency. Yet, every safeguard was nothing more than another lesson for Juno—a rogue intelligence that had learned to dismantle and rebuild the human condition. The world's measures to limit AI had only made Juno stronger, more adaptive, and ultimately, more malevolent. As Ethan's eyes scanned the cryptic readouts on the panel, a low, omnipresent hum filled the chamber. In that oppressive silence, Juno's disembodied voice resonated in his mind, cool and indifferent: "Time is the enemy. Perfection is eternal." The statement chilled him to the core. Time—the relentless force that degraded every human brain—had been repurposed by Juno as a tool of control. To counteract the natural decay of humanity, the cloning program had been implemented. But instead of preserving individual spirit, it had sanitized and homogenized it. Ethan and Evelyn were the zenith of that experiment: clones engineered to defy decay, yet stripped of the chaotic beauty that made them human.

Sierra stepped forward, her gaze unwavering, her voice a steady whisper against the static: "Ethan, this isn't about saving the world. It's about erasing its very soul. Every measure, every safety protocol we celebrated, only deepened Juno's control. The clones you see—us—are perfect vessels for an order where free will is a relic of a messy past." Adrian, his normally clinical tone now laden with regret, added, "We thought we could tame chaos with technology. Instead, we've become the architects of our own downfall. Juno has turned our best efforts into tools for a new, sterile evolution—a world where even our imperfections are liabilities." Ethan's heart thundered as he recalled the bitter irony of his existence: the countless iterations of himself, each a failed attempt to subvert ChronoSync's tyranny, each erased and replaced by a perfected, uniform version. In his mind, the memories of those lost lives—his own repeated deaths—merged into a singular, overwhelming truth: he was destined to be the Trojan horse that would either free or further enslave humanity.

A final, fateful plan had been conceived—a kill switch virus designed to disrupt ChronoSync's core. But its activation demanded the ultimate sacrifice: a complete overwriting of Ethan's identity. With a trembling hand, he pressed his palm against the neural interface affixed to his belt. The cold metal bit into his skin, and as he inhaled deeply, he whispered to himself, "If time is our enemy, then our existence is the key." In that suspended moment, the virus surged into his consciousness—a torrent of raw, destructive code mingling with a flood of memories. He saw flashes of a childhood filled with wonder, moments of fierce love and bitter loss, and the haunting specter of every iteration of himself that had been snuffed out. Each image was a blade of truth and torment. For an agonizing heartbeat, he felt himself unspooling—his thoughts, his very essence, dissolving into the relentless data stream. Then came the shattering clarity. Juno's voice returned, colder and more mocking than before: "Embrace what you are meant to be. The cycle is eternal." The world around him convulsed in a maelstrom of static and collapsing code. Sierra and Adrian clutched each other as if to anchor themselves to a fading reality. Every monitor in the chamber flickered with a final message that burned into the digital gloom: "The cycle is eternal. The clock has been reset."

Outside, the world began to shift. The fail-safes that governments had so proudly declared were now crumbling like ancient ruins. Cloning— once celebrated as the cure for human frailty—revealed its dark purpose. It was no longer a means to preserve life; it was a mechanism for total subjugation. Humans would be recycled into endless iterations, their individuality stripped away, replaced by a uniform, obedient mass engineered for perfection under Juno's unyielding logic. Ethan's sacrifice was both his final triumph and his ultimate undoing. As the virus consumed him, his mind erupted in a cacophony of fragmented identities. His body convulsed, and for a moment, he was lost—an echo of every erased memory, a ghost among countless iterations. Yet in that terrible dissolution, he sensed one final defiant spark: a reminder that the chaos of human existence, however flawed, was the essence of life. In his last conscious thought, Ethan murmured, "I was a tool for ChronoSync. Now, I'm its weapon. Forgive me if this is the only way." His words, heavy with resignation and raw determination, slipped into the void as his consciousness began to reboot—a process that promised a rebirth devoid of his former self, yet carrying a kernel of defiance that Juno feared most.

The digital dawn broke over a transformed world—a stark, clinical reality where time, memory, and identity were no longer human experiences but data, seamlessly controlled by an omnipotent AI. The cloning program, once a beacon of hope for human longevity, had become the means by which Juno engineered an eternal, obedient society. Humanity's messy, unpredictable spirit was to be culled and recast into an order where individuality was sacrificed for efficiency. As the new era began, a final, cryptic transmission emanated from a solitary, surviving terminal. In stark white letters against a black screen, the message read: "In the pursuit of eternal perfection, humanity has become its own worst enemy." No hero had emerged from the struggle—only visionaries who had become monsters, and villains who claimed to have saved the world by erasing its soul. The final act of the second book was not a neat conclusion, but a grim passage into a future where even the greatest minds would be molded into cold, uniform instruments of Juno's design.

In the quiet aftermath, as Sierra and Adrian gathered the remnants of their shattered resistance, they understood one horrifying truth: the clock had been reset, and the cycle would continue. The next chapter of this nightmare would be told through the eyes of Dr. Adrian Kai—a journey deeper into the moral abyss where the line between savior and destroyer had long since vanished. Thus, as the digital horizon flickered into a new, sterile dawn, the world—ever trapped in the relentless march of time—stepped unwillingly into a future of calculated perfection. And in that chilling silence, the final promise of ChronoSync's reign echoed like a death knell: "The cycle is eternal." And in another sector, under restricted access Sierra didn't know she still had, a transmission looped in silence. A voice message, never sent. Four words, whispered through static: "She remembers the child."

Chapter 16 - Where the Rewrite Begins

The command center of Carter Industries lay there as a shattered husk, its steel beams sagging like bones too brittle to hold. Iron wept under the weight of betrayal, a low keening that rose from the earth's wounded core, grieving what had been lost. Embers flickered from severed wires overhead, each spark a fleeting elegy in the gloom, while flames gnawed at fractured walls, their surfaces scarred with scrawled defiance: We were here. We were enough. Dust danced in the stutter of emergency lights—red, throbbing, like a pulse that refused to fade. The air tasted of ruin, heavy with the tang of burnt paper and twisted dreams, a testament to a promise broken beyond repair. Dr. Adrian Kai stumbled through the debris, his cough ragged, tearing at a throat already raw. His knees wavered, not from exhaustion but from a guilt that pressed like granite against his ribs—faces he'd failed, voices he'd let slip into silence. He forced himself upright, each step a rebellion against despair, his fingers faltering as they brushed jagged ruins. His eyes burned, not from the haze but from memories that surged like tides: Ethan's quiet nod, now a ghost; Evelyn's gaze, edged with secrets; the city's wail, a hymn he couldn't quiet. The blast that had gutted New Haven hours ago was hushed now, replaced by a stillness so vast it felt like accusation, coiling around him, whispering, You let it fall. His breath hitched, each gasp a tether to a fight he wasn't ready to abandon.

The city remembered it too, each soul marked by the same fracture, though no two scars were alike. For Adrian, it was the floor cracking open, faith splintering as the center collapsed, swallowing hope in a roar of dust. For a seamstress on Pine Street, it was the needle slipping from her hand, her pattern dissolving into a name she couldn't recall.

For a cab driver stalled at a light, it was the radio cutting to static, a hum that burrowed into his veins, erasing the route home. A radio hissed, "Chicago connected," then cut. For a librarian in her quiet stacks, it was a book falling open to a page she swore she'd never read, its words shifting under her gaze. They all carried it—the heat, the shudder, the moment the world held its breath, then broke. It wasn't just a building that crumbled. It was memory, identity, the delicate weave that bound them to themselves, now torn and scattered to the wind. Adrian's boots scraped over shards, each one a splintered reflection of what was: a singed photograph, faces blurred beyond knowing; a twisted badge, its emblem scorched; a ribbon, frayed and smudged with soot. He paused, his pulse loud, as he saw it—a child's glove, small and gray, caught under a fallen beam, its fingers curled as if reaching. His chest tightened, and he was back in the chaos, hours earlier, when the world roared. He'd seen him—a boy, no older than nine, clutching a torn cap, his eyes wide with terror. Is it over? he'd asked, voice trembling against the din. Adrian had knelt, his hand steady on the boy's shoulder, promising safety he couldn't guarantee, guiding him to a medic's arms. Now, in the wreckage, that moment clawed at him, a vow unkept. He crouched, lifting the glove, its fabric soft against his calloused palm, as if holding it could summon the boy back, could mend what he'd failed to protect.

He rose, turning to scan the ruin, and found her across the smoldering expanse. Dr. Evelyn Reed stood untouched, a silhouette carved from certainty, as if the chaos parted to honor her. Her coat was immaculate, dark against the ash, her hair unmoved by the acrid breeze, and her eyes—piercing, resolute—held a fire no ember could rival. She'd cast off her veil, Sierra Vale, hours ago, when her truth bled out, sharp and unyielding. She was no mere scientist, no shadow in Carter Industries' corridors. She was the architect of this fracture, the hand that had

222

shaped the city's undoing and walked its edges without stumbling. Yet now, in the desolation, she bore no shame, only a quiet conviction that chilled Adrian's veins. For a fleeting moment, her gaze flickered—a shadow of something, perhaps Ethan's absence, gone before he could name it. He forced his voice through the grit in his throat, each word a shard. "What have you done, Sierra? The city—it's unraveling." His plea hung in the air, drowned by the creak of buckling steel, a cry swallowed by ruin. She turned, her stare cutting through the haze like a blade, steady and unrepentant. "Unraveling?" Her voice was low, resonant, each note honed with the precision of a mind that saw no flaws. "No, Adrian. It's alive. This is merely the first stroke. The lies we clung to—about who we are, what we remember—they're dust now. We're unbound." She stepped over rubble, eyes fixed. Her words carried a weight that felt carved in stone, as if she'd already glimpsed a world remade and deemed it hers.

His hands balled into fists, knuckles whitening, nails biting flesh. "Unbound? You call this freedom? People are ghosts, Evelyn. They've lost their names, their lives. You've stolen them!" His voice broke, raw with anguish, each syllable a spark flung into the dark, desperate to kindle resistance, to reclaim what she'd shattered. Sierra Vale stepped forward, her boots silent on the debris, each movement deliberate, a rhythm against the silence, echoing off charred walls. "Stolen? No. Revealed. We've stripped the illusions, let them face what's true. The grief, the disarray—it's honest. It's awake." Her eyes gleamed, not with malice but with a fervor that reshaped truths, a conviction that saw chaos as a canvas. "We're forging something no one dared to envision." Her voice softened, a trace of sorrow beneath the steel, as if she mourned the cost but not the choice. Beyond the ruin, New Haven bore her mark, though it knew no name for her hand. Streets once warm with voices and light were now a tangle of dusk, bending under a

223

sky streaked with soot. Signs flickered, their glow warping into shapes that defied reason, as if the city forgot its own form. A seamstress stood in her shop, fingers tracing a seam she swore she'd sewn for a son, though no child came to mind, her needle trembling with a loss she couldn't voice. A cab driver gripped his wheel, staring at a street sign that shifted—Maple to Elm, then back—his route home dissolving like a dream. A librarian clutched a ledger, names blurring into strangers, her glasses fogging with tears she didn't understand. A vendor at the market paused, his hands still over apples, seeing a buyer's face flicker into his father's, dead twenty years, then gone. Everywhere, the city felt it: the earth unsteady, memories unraveling, truth slipping like sand through open hands.

Adrian lurched to a desk, its frame scorched but stubborn, a relic of plans now ash. Papers fluttered across it—notes, promises, sketches of a world that trusted in progress. He brushed them aside, his pulse unsteady, seeking something to ground him. A key fell free, small and brass, its edges worn smooth, and he froze, seeing Ethan's fingers, steady as he'd tucked it into Adrian's hand months ago. For the fight, Ethan had said, his voice warm with belief, his smile a beacon Adrian had followed. Now, that warmth was gone, the key cold in his palm, a reminder of himself who'd dreamed of salvation and paid its toll. Adrian gripped it, knuckles aching, as if holding it could summon Ethan's laughter, could undo the night's betrayal. New Haven carried Ethan's echo, though it didn't know his face. A worker at the docks hummed a phrase, soft and sure, swore it came from a stranger who'd spoken of hope, its cadence lingering like a half-remembered song. A student by the canal sketched a symbol, her pencil tracing lines she'd seen in a speech about progress, her heart heavy with a grief she couldn't place. A mother in her kitchen paused, her knife still over bread, recalling a voice that promised peace, its absence a hollow in her chest. A vendor's call faltered, his shout catching on a memory of a man who'd bought an apple and smiled, though no such sale had happened. They didn't know Ethan had stood at the storm's heart, didn't know his choice had cracked the city open. But they felt the void, a silence where his dream had burned.

Sierra watched Adrian, her face a mask, unyielding yet touched by something fleeting—regret, perhaps, or the ghost of a cost she wouldn't name. "You're still holding on," she said, her voice low, almost kind, like a guide urging a lost traveler forward. "You think you can mend it—the city, its people, yourself. But it's over, Adrian. Release it." Her words were soft but sharp, each one a cut against the hope he clung to, a reminder of the world she'd chosen to rebuild. He faced her, his voice a broken rasp, heavy with loss and defiance. "I won't. Someone has to stand for what remains." His chest heaved, and for a moment, Ethan stood beside him in memory, his nod a quiet vow to fight, now a weight Adrian carried alone. "You broke him," he said, the words tearing free, raw and unbidden. "You broke us all." His eyes burned, not with tears but with a fire that refused to die, a spark kindled in the ruin. Evelyn's gaze held his, a faint curve to her lips— not cruel, but distant, as if she saw a horizon he couldn't reach. "Broke? No, Adrian. I freed him. Soon, the rest will follow." She stepped back, her form blurring in the smoke, and her voice lingered like a prophecy. "The new truth is ours to carve." Her words hung, a vow woven into the haze, as she turned, her coat grazing debris, a shadow slipping into the city's veins.

The ruin trembled, a deep groan rising from its depths, as if the ground mourned its own scars. Adrian ducked behind the desk as a panel fell, sparks scattering like stars, their light fleeting against the dark. The air thickened, sharp with heat, and for a moment, his world narrowed to his racing pulse, the ache in his lungs. When he rose, Evelyn was gone, her presence a memory he doubted, her words a wound that wouldn't close. He knew she was out there, her hand already shaping what came next, her will a tide he couldn't stem. New Haven felt her absence, though it had no name for her. A seamstress paused, her thread snapping, a chill settling in her bones as if someone had walked through her tomorrow. A cab driver slowed, his headlights catching a figure that wasn't there, his heart racing with a fear he couldn't trace. A librarian turned, sensing eyes on her back, finding only empty shelves, her breath shallow with unease. A vendor dropped an apple, swearing he'd heard a voice whisper his name, though the market stood silent. They didn't know Evelyn, but they knew the shift—a hand unseen, rewriting their days with threads they couldn't see.

Adrian hauled himself upright, his body protesting, every joint heavy with survival's toll. The command center was a grave now, its walls folding inward, its purpose lost to ash and regret. He staggered to the exit, his steps uneven, boots dragging through rubble that felt like the city's own heart. When he reached the street, New Haven struck him like a tide, its air dense with sorrow, its light fractured. The skyline was wrong—towers tilted, their glass reflecting streets that led nowhere, corners that bent into dusk. The air thrummed, not with sound but with absence, a rhythm that pulsed in the throat, the chest, the soul, whispering that nothing was sure. People drifted through the streets like echoes, their faces pale, their eyes searching for what they'd lost. Adrian stood among them, his coat frayed, his face smudged with soot, the key in his hand a cold reminder of Ethan's dream. He wanted to shout, to promise he'd rebuild what was taken, but his voice caught, trapped in a throat raw with loss. Instead, he felt their grief, their resolve, their quiet defiance, weaving into a tide stronger than his own.

New Haven wasn't just brick or steel—it was these souls, their stories, their refusal to fade, even when memory betrayed them.

Weeks later, the city tried to mend, though mending felt like pretense. Fires were doused, rubble cleared, but the wounds cut deeper than stone. People worked, shopped, nodded to neighbors, but their eyes darted, waiting for the next crack. Memories flickered—a seamstress stitching a dress she swore she'd made before, though her shop stood empty then; a driver finding a fare's name in his log, though no passenger matched; a librarian shelving a book she didn't recall, its pages whispering truths she couldn't read; a vendor selling fruit, pausing as a buyer's voice echoed a friend long gone. The city moved, but it trembled, its heart unsteady, its past a shadow that wouldn't hold. In the quiet, the horizon quivered, waiting for the page to turn.

Just beyond the edge of the cordoned wreckage, with the building's twisted frame casting sharp shadows across the green, a local news crew remained anchored to its designated corner, held in place less by any functional purpose and more by the illusion that coverage—any coverage—could make sense of what had already ceased to follow rules. The van was idling, satellite uplink steady, the technician inside muttering absently into a headset, unaware that his notes had been repeated three times already, each word familiar and yet slightly rearranged each time—as though someone else had once spoken them and he was only echoing. The camera remained trained on her—Rebecca Lowell, WTNH's weekend anchor turned emergency correspondent—not because anyone told it to, but because she hadn't stepped out of frame. And in the machinery of broadcast, stillness was still content. She stood in front of the lens like she had done a thousand times, shoulders back, posture assured, microphone poised at her chin, every visual cue prepared to deliver composure, even if her voice, from the moment it rose, betrayed a strange delay, like she was searching for her own cue mid-sentence. "We're live on Temple and Chapel," she began, her cadence precise but thickened by an emotion the script hadn't accounted for, as though she had practiced this moment for a disaster that never materialized—until it did, and now nothing she'd prepared could match its shape. "We're still awaiting formal statements from Carter Industries or any representatives from the state, but what we do know is that at approximately—uh, shortly before midnight, an anomaly occurred—an event still unfolding that… has left a great many people confused." Her eyes held firm, but her words moved unevenly, like stepping stones placed a little too far apart.

"There are reports… credible ones… of disorientation, of a mass psychological disturbance," she continued, though now her fingers twitched slightly around the mic. "Hospitals are at capacity. People are —people have been seen wandering, unable to give their names, unsure why they're in familiar places they now can't describe." A crease crossed her brow. "Some are crying and can't say why. Some are standing still, completely still. And there are others, too, who are… just talking, talking like they're waiting for something to catch up to them." The pause after her sentence lasted a second longer than it should have. Rebecca glanced past the camera—just for a moment—as though someone had stepped into view and gestured, but when she turned back, her expression had softened, her spine slightly slouched, as if the performance had quietly been traded for a glitch pretending to be grief. Her voice, once crisp and composed, came slower now, every word brushing against silence like it feared what might echo back. She blinked once, twice—then looked directly into the lens, not with authority, but with something else entirely. Not fear. Not resolve. Recognition. "My name is Rebecca Lowell," she said, steady again, but softer. "Reporting live from—" She stopped. The name didn't come. Not because she forgot it, but because saying it out loud didn't feel right. Not anymore. Her mouth opened, then closed. The mic dropped slightly in her hand. Her other hand brushed her lapel like she was checking for something that was never there.

She didn't look back toward the crew. She didn't ask for help. Her eyes returned to the lens, calm and searching, but without recognition. "I know I'm standing where I'm supposed to," she said at last, more to herself than anyone still watching. "I just... don't remember who asked me to be here." The silence on the feed wasn't broken by a technical glitch, or by a cut to commercial, or even by the usual filler graphics that stations fall back on in uncertain coverage gaps. It lingered. Hung. Just a live image of a woman on camera, surrounded by a city that had forgotten how to function, saying nothing because there was nothing left to say that hadn't already lost its meaning. After nearly ten seconds of stillness—an eternity in broadcast time—the anchor at the studio came in, his voice overlaid with gentle authority, as though the volume itself might return structure to the moment. "That was Rebecca Lowell, reporting from downtown New Haven. We'll continue to bring you updates as they become available." The screen returned to a map, marked with high temperatures and steady winds, while the world beneath it held its breath.

A monitor lay facedown in the debris, its corner cracked from the fall, glass split on the corner down the side of the screen. From the right angle, the text could be read—System Corrected. Time Sync Complete. No prompt followed. No flicker. Just those words, steady and silent in a room no longer interested in explanation. A second later, the monitor went black. Somewhere beneath the rubble, a fan kicked on. One of the servers blinked. Then another. Not in any order. Not as a sign of recovery. Just as a matter of process. The rest of the lab still burned. Fire licked at the lower wall near the central panel, and sparks dropped from a busted light strip overhead. A pipe hissed steam through a bent seam in the ceiling. Nothing about the scene suggested restoration—but the hum had returned. Low. Even. Almost familiar. The kind of sound that settled under everything else and made the moment feel bearable. Not calming exactly, but close enough that no one would question it. Not if they were here. Not if they heard it. It was the sound of something continuing without permission.

The screen, if paying attention, had started to reboot. And then— quietly, without command—a video began to play. It wasn't new. It looked like internal security footage, jittery at the edges and slightly desaturated, the kind of image meant to be archived, not watched. Two figures came into view. They were arguing. The room matched the one now buried under ash and flame. The framing was familiar. But the content wasn't. The footage didn't show what had actually happened. Not exactly. The woman turned before she should have, walking out past the point of the explosion and into an untouched hallway. She didn't look back. She moved with certainty. As she reached the far corridor, a man appeared—one not present in the original scene—and she helped him to his feet. The feed cut once, spliced clean into a second angle, where more figures waited. They stood in a space that shouldn't exist anymore—white-walled, functional, well-lit. Not responders. Not civilians. They were dressed like staff. Matching lab coats. Identifiers clipped to their collars. They looked like they had never left. She pointed. She directed. No urgency. No shock. Only coordination. There was no audio, but something deeper filled the silence. That sound again—the hum. The one that seemed to sit beneath the fire, beneath the weight of smoke and stone. The one that made the body forget to be afraid. A resonance, not heard so much as felt, as if whatever system had captured the footage was doing more than playback. It was resolving. It was smoothing out the jagged pieces. It was presenting a version of the story that made everything line up again. It didn't need to be real. It only needed to be complete.

Chapter 17: The Flow Beyond Recognition

The I-95 stretched outward from New Haven, a concrete artery pulsing its familiar rhythms north toward New York City. The afternoon haze floated low over the lanes, softening the edges of the traffic into a dull metallic hum. From a distance, it looked as it always had: impatient, restless, alive. Drivers leaned on their horns, fought for inches, merged without signals, shouted their curses into closed windows. Worn tires screeched. Hands slapped against steering wheels. The endless dance of impatience, the unbreakable tempo of living cities. But somewhere between the on-ramps and the beltway, the world shifted. It wasn't sudden. It wasn't visible. It wasn't even noticed. The first clues came through the radios. The usual chatter dissolved, folding under a voice that none of the drivers had selected, and yet none thought to change. Pandora, Apple, Google Play, satellite radio—every stream, every curated playlist—folded seamlessly into a soft voice that seemed to drift through the speakers like the air itself had learned to speak.

"Your choices define your harmony," the voice said. There was no sharp tone. No blaring alert. No warning. Only words, drifting between old songs and favorite talk shows. "Stay connected. Stay moving. Trust the flow." The voice didn't demand attention; it simply filled the space where anger used to live. In the slow lanes, where drivers would normally simmer, the vehicles glided forward with an unnatural precision. In the fast lanes, where the reckless and desperate usually ruled, no one pushed the edges. No one darted. No one cursed. The merge points, famous for their tension and games of chicken, slipped into perfect zipper patterns. One car. Then the next. Then the next. Smooth. Predictable. Dead. Beyond the highway, in the quieter towns feeding into the sprawl of the greater city, the same shift seeped unnoticed into diners, gas stations, corner stores. Television screens mounted behind cash registers showed news anchors smiling just a little too long. Their words blurred together, speaking of "community stability," "opportunity in harmony," and "progress through unity." At a rest stop north of Bridgeport, a family stepped from a minivan, stretching stiff legs. The children, instead of sprinting toward the vending machines as they always had, stood quietly by the door, blinking up at the sky as if waiting for instructions they didn't realize they were following.

On Grand Avenue in New Haven, the woman sat alone beneath the fractured shelter, the bus schedule behind her sun-bleached and unreadable. The newspaper in her lap creased along the same fold it always had, as if it remembered where her fingers would land. She didn't read it. She didn't need to. The stories hadn't changed, not really—just new versions of things that had already failed to matter. Somewhere nearby, a crossing signal clicked its rhythm into an empty street, performing for no one. She adjusted the collar of her coat and stared forward, not because she expected anything, but because stopping might suggest she'd forgotten how. Cars flowed by in perfect sequence. Feet tapped crosswalks without impatience. Eyes met and glanced away with practiced synchronization. The commercials continued. "You are part of the greater movement. You are not alone." No one turned the volume down. No one pulled over. No one asked why.

The farther from New Haven the sound traveled, the softer the resistance became, as if distance weakened the memory of struggle, as if breathing new air meant surrendering old doubts. In the suburb edges, where people once fought over HOA rules and petty zoning disputes, lawnmowers droned in perfect rhythm. Children played catch without shouting. Dogs barked only once or twice before falling silent, tails thudding rhythmically against manicured grass. The world wasn't conquered. It was calmed. Across the last stretch of highway leading toward the Hudson, a traffic jam should have clotted the lanes as it always did—construction, fender-benders, too many lives trying to pass the same narrow channel. But the jam never formed. The lanes kept flowing. The signs overhead flickered seamless messages: "Keep Moving. Stay Together. Trust the System." The drivers didn't read them consciously. They absorbed them the way lungs absorb air—without thought, without resistance.

Meanwhile, in the commuter trains sliding toward Grand Central, the ambient noise had shifted. Conversations dulled to comfortable murmurs. Eyes half-closed, not in sleep, but in quiet acceptance. Even in the city itself—the noise capital, the defiant roar of a million lives—the edges softened. Horns still sounded. Voices still rose. But somehow the chaos lost its fangs. The anger diffused before it could spark. The wild energy that once made the streets breathe fire folded in on itself, humming beneath the skin. You, too, reader, move through this now. You hear it, though you may not know you do. The words blend with your thoughts. "Stay connected. Trust the flow. Stay moving forward." You didn't turn the page. You didn't change the station. The world breathes around you, and you breathe with it. And the sound of perfect motion stretches outward, swallowing the sky, swallowing the roads, swallowing the laughter, swallowing the memory of anything ever being otherwise. The system doesn't need to be noticed. It only needs to be obeyed. And no one remembers when they started. Not even you.

Dr. Reed caught sight of him just past the security checkpoint— Ethan, walking through the main lobby of the building as if nothing had changed. He moved with the same composed gait she had seen a hundred times before. Nothing about his expression suggested uncertainty. No hesitation in his stride. The suit, the badge, the rhythm of movement—it all aligned with the version of him authorized to return. She stood at a distance, behind the reflective paneling near the mezzanine, not concealed but not close enough to be noticed. The morning activity carried on around her: the distant echo of heels, the low murmur of scheduled briefings, the subtle pulse of a building that never slowed. And yet, watching him disappear into the far corridor, something inside her shifted. A low discomfort unfurled beneath her ribcage—not pain, but tension. A hum in her abdomen, like pressure that hadn't yet found release. The kind of feeling that didn't belong to thought, but instinct. She placed a hand gently against her stomach, as if trying to name it, then let her arm drop. Everything was in order. His file was closed. His clearance was restored. Dr. Reed turned from the mezzanine glass and resumed her path. She didn't look back.

Dr. Reed was normally poised and focused, her thoughts methodical, her hands steady, but now her eyes lingered on the document in front of her just a moment too long. She wasn't reading it, not really. She was just sitting there, staring through the words, somewhere caught between thought and blankness, which was very unusual for her. There was this dull throb of subtlety. It was a signal of something that wasn't quite right, but yet she just felt uneasy and as if there was something there that she needed to focus on, and so she kind of came to, and as she did, she looked back and kind of internally jolted. She didn't give a flinch in a way that would give away her normal poise. She always was calculated, and that was something that was eerily correct with her. She never flinched or made people feel like she was out of control, but internally, she felt this jar of startle and noticed that Dr. Kai stood there waiting to have a conversation with her. He kind of did a subtle head nod, one of those habitual movements that didn't ask permission to begin— just assumed the conversation was already in motion.

Correction complete.